The

MW01138725

Company Business

(A Paranormal Snapshot)

By Sherry A. Burton

 Dorry Press

Also by Sherry A. Burton

The Orphan Train Saga

Discovery (book one)
Shameless (book two)
Treachery (book three)
Guardian (book four)
Loyal (book five)
Patience (book six)
Endurance (book seven)

Orphan Train Extras

Ezra's Story

Jerry McNeal Series (Also in Audio)

Always Faithful (book one)
Ghostly Guidance (book two)
Rambling Spirit (book three)
Chosen Path (book four)
Port Hope (book five)
Cold Case (book six)
Wicked Winds (book seven)
Mystic Angel (book eight)
Uncanny Coincidence (book nine)
Chesapeake Chaos (book ten)
Village Shenanigans (book eleven)
Special Delivery (book twelve)
Spirit of Deadwood (a full-length novel, book thirteen)
Star Treatment (book fourteen)
Merry Me (book fifteen)
Hidden Treasures (book sixteen)
Company Business (book seventeen)
Dearly Departed (book eighteen)

The Jerry McNeal Series
Company Business

By Sherry A. Burton

Copyright 2024
The Jerry McNeal Series: Company Business
By Sherry A. Burton
Published by Dorry Press
Edited and Formatted by BZHercules.com
Cover by Laura J. Prevost @laurajprevostphotography
Proofread by Latisha Rich

All rights reserved. No part of this book may be reproduced in any form or by any electronic or mechanical means, including information storage and retrieval systems—except in the case of brief quotations embodied in critical articles or reviews—without permission in writing from the author at Sherryaburton@outlook.com. This book is a work of fiction. The characters, events, and places portrayed in this book are products of the author's imagination and are either fictitious or are used fictitiously. Any similarity to real persons, living or dead, is purely coincidental and not intended by the author.

For more information on the author and her works, and to sign up for the newsletter, please see www.SherryABurton.com

A special thanks to

I will forever be grateful to my mom, who insisted the dog stay in the series.

To my hubby, thanks for helping me stay in the writing chair.

To my editor, Beth, for allowing me to keep my voice.

To Laura, for the fantastic covers.

To my beta readers for giving the books an early read.

To my proofreader, Latisha Rich, for the extra set of eyes.

To my fans, for the continued support.

Lastly, to my "writing voices," thank you for all the incredible ideas!

Chapter One

Ground rules. Everyone should have them. They could be as simple as making one's bed immediately upon waking. Or, perhaps, not taking phone calls from work after a certain hour. Some tend to take things a step further by inflicting their ground rules on others. Parents are particularly good at that. In his younger years, Jerry's mother wouldn't tolerate him talking about spirits at the table. His father took things a bit further, forbidding Jerry to talk about spirits altogether. Though he didn't realize it at the time, his parents' refusal was due to the fear of the unknown.

Now that he was grown, Jerry had his own ground rules, the first of which was that he did not talk with spirits until after he'd had his first cup of coffee each day. While it was good to have a motto to live by, it was a good idea to reevaluate those rules from time to time.

These days, his parents both eagerly listened to whatever he told them about the spirit world, and he himself found it necessary to bend his ground rules on occasion. This was precisely what he was doing at present since his dearly departed grandmother decided to appear in the early hours to have a chat with him before the rest of the spirit community decided to drop in with their list of demands.

Gunter stood while Jerry eased his way out of bed. Jerry spoke to the dog using his mind. *It's okay, boy. We're just going to be on the other side of that wall. Don't let any of the spirits disturb her.*

Gunter yawned and moved into the spot next to April that Jerry had just vacated.

Lucky dog. For a moment, Jerry thought about telling his grandmother she'd have to wait. *I'll meet you in the kitchen*, he said so only she could hear.

She raised a brow.

I don't care if you're a spirit; I'd still like a little privacy. He waited for her to leave then pulled on his jeans and followed her out of the room.

"I made coffee," Granny said, leading the way into the kitchen of the small vacation house they'd rented in DuBois, Pennsylvania.

This was a new one. Jerry eyed the coffee pot suspiciously.

Granny laughed a lighthearted laugh. "Jerry

Carter McNeal, you look as if you think I'm trying to poison you."

Jerry walked to the counter and poured himself a cup. Sniffing the contents, he took a sip. "It's good."

Granny chuckled once more. "Of course it is. April made it before turning in last night. All I had to do was push a button."

Jerry leaned against the counter. "I don't suppose there are any cinnamon rolls in the oven?"

"No, but I can get some if you'd like."

Jerry shook his head. "No, coffee will do for now."

"How's April handling her newfound gift?" Granny asked, referring to April's ability to hear and speak with spirits.

Jerry walked to the living room and sat on the sofa. "I don't think she's had time to fully process things."

"How long are you staying?"

Jerry sighed an exasperated sigh. "We hadn't planned on staying at all. When the spirits showed up, April thought it would be easier to deal with them here."

"You didn't tell her they could find you wherever you go?"

Jerry pulled the lever to raise the footrest and crossed his ankles. "She knows that. I figured since we didn't have anywhere to be, we could take a few days for things to settle down."

Granny arched an eyebrow. "How's that working out for you?"

Jerry smiled. "It's not. She and Max concocted this plan to catalog the spirits and their requests. That would allow April to work through each case as she finds time. But for every spirit she and Max catalog, two more show up."

"That's because each spirit will tell two spirits, who tell two spirits," Granny agreed.

Jerry wasn't convinced. "What do you know about the Spirit Pipeline?"

"I know whoever told you about it has a big mouth," Granny said heatedly.

"I know you think I need to make my own way, but it isn't as if I can Google this stuff," Jerry said. Knowing his grandmother's anger wasn't directed at him, he decided to push the issue. "Am I wrong, or has something changed?"

"You mean besides the fact April is now aware of her gift? Does her having it bother you?"

"Of course not." Jerry chuckled. "Though I think Max is still on the fence."

"Oh, how come?"

"She's thirteen," Jerry said by way of explanation. "Would you have wanted your mother to be privy to all your thoughts at that age?"

"Max knows she can block her."

"She knows. She just hasn't had to do it before. Neither have I." Jerry shrugged. "April's better with hearing spirits. Hearing me and Max still seems to be hit or miss. It's not that any of us have anything to hide, but a little privacy goes a long way. This is new to all of us. I'm sure we'll figure it out."

"Of course you will," Granny agreed. "You didn't develop your gifts overnight."

Jerry frowned. "I was born with my gifts."

"Yes, but just because you had them doesn't mean you knew what to do with them. We both know you were running from them up until a couple of years ago."

Jerry glanced at the bedroom. "I hope it doesn't take April that long to figure it out."

"Is she having trouble with this?" Granny asked.

"Yes and no," Jerry replied.

"I'm going to need a little more than that if you expect me to help."

"Unlike me, April is jumping in with both feet. I didn't realize it, but she's felt a little lost lately. I do my thing and Max does hers, but April hasn't had a thing."

"Until now," Granny replied.

"Exactly. So she's running with it, and it's consuming her every waking hour."

"Jerry McNeal, do I detect a note of jealousy?"

"I'm not jealous," Jerry answered truthfully. "I just want her to set some boundaries, which she's finding difficult to do with the number of requests she's receiving. That's why I asked about the Spirit

Pipeline. This isn't normal, this is…"

Granny appeared beside him and patted his hand. "There is nothing nefarious about this, Jerry. April's gift is big news on this side."

Jerry welcomed the touch. "April is still honing her gift. What makes her so special? You know why I think she's special, but why does she mean so much to the spirit world as opposed to, say, Susie or Savannah?"

"Susie and Savannah don't have cheerleaders," Granny said softly.

"I'm not following you."

Granny pulled back her hand and worried them in front of her stomach.

Jerry sat his cup on the coaster and turned to face her. "I was right. You know something!"

Granny lifted her hands in front of her, and when she did, a newspaper appeared.

Jerry leaned close, reading the headline. *Michigan Woman April Buchanan Travels to Pennsylvania and Finds New Calling.* A tingle raced along the nape of his neck. "What is this?"

"A newspaper."

Jerry forced himself to remain calm. "I know it's a newspaper. Who's responsible for its content?"

Granny folded the paper across her lap. "Why, the editor, of course."

Jerry pushed off the couch and placed a finger at the side of his eye to still a twitch. "Betty Lou, you've been hanging around with Bunny too long," he said, pacing the floor.

At the mention of Bunny, the spirit appeared. Dressed conservatively in black pants and a white shirt, she had a pencil tucked behind her ear and wore a white hat with a black band circling the brim. Her shirt sleeves were rolled to the elbow and spotted with ink. She glanced at the newspaper and clapped her hands. "Oh, goodie, you're reading the *Spirit Pipeline*."

Jerry cleared his throat.

Bunny turned, saw him standing there, and gulped. "Oh, dear. I guess the cat's out of the bag."

Jerry nodded to the newspaper. "You're telling me you're the one responsible for that?"

Bunny beamed a wide grin. "Oh yes. The *Spirit Pipeline* is all the rage. Everyone wants a copy. Why, I can't print them fast enough."

"So, it is a newspaper? Teddy said it was a frequency."

"Teddy?"

"The spirit from the house," Granny interjected.

"Oh, you mean Theodore," Bunny mused. "He must not have opted for the paper copy."

"I don't give care what subscription he chose," Jerry said heatedly. "You need to leave my family out of your tabloid."

Instantly, Gunter appeared at his side.

Bunny's eyes widened. "Oh, no, Jerry, you've

got it all wrong. The *Spirit Pipeline* is more than just a respectable news source. We put out special editions whenever there is a big event. And it's not just in print; it's available as a download. Why, we had over a billion downloads when Betty died."

Jerry glanced at his grandmother. "A billion?"

Granny chuckled. "I appreciate that you think I'm that newsworthy, but she means Betty White."

"Her death was big news," Bunny said, bobbing her head. "We hadn't had that many downloads since Elvis crossed over."

Even though he knew better than to encourage her, Jerry couldn't resist asking, "You're saying you were digital in 1977?"

This evoked another head bob from the spirit. "Oh yes, we get all the good inventions first. It helps to make sure things work before we share them with the living."

"You're saying spirits give us ideas? What about the inventions that don't work?"

Bunny made a tsking noise with her tongue. "You're a smart man, Jer. I'm sure you know that not all spirits follow the rules. You'd be gobsmacked at the number who leak things before making sure the information is solid."

Jerry looked at his grandmother. "Is she for real?"

Granny shrugged. "Bunny is as real as I am."

"I was asking if what she's saying is true?"

Bunny puffed her chest. "Of course it's true. Everyone is given something from their guardian angels. Not everyone decides to act on it."

Jerry rocked back on his heels. "I'm pretty sure I would have known if a spirit ever handed me the plans for an invention."

Bunny waved him off. "Oh, it's not only inventions. Have you ever heard someone say they'd like to skydive? Or how about someone who says, 'I've always wanted to write a book'? Those are gifts from their guardian angel."

"How is skydiving and writing a book the same as getting credited for an invention?"

"It's not about the credit; it's about the experience and the joy one gets from accomplishing a task or conquering a fear. Some act on the gift, others do not. It's their choice, after all, but some spirits get a little crabby if their ideas keep getting thwarted and might not be so eager to offer their assistance after that. Oh, they'll still help their charge out, but a spirit gets spurned enough times, and they might not be as likely to go over and above to see them happy."

Something had been bugging him about the whole conversation. He eyed the spirit, trying to see what was different.

Bunny smiled a brilliant pink smile. "A man leers at a dame like that, and they'd better expect to get either slapped or kissed," she said and licked her lips.

Gunter groaned.

Jerry forced a blank stare while inwardly experiencing a full-body shiver. "I wasn't leering at you. I was trying to see what changed."

A fleeting frown crossed her face. "What do you mean, changed?"

"You're different." *Don't say it, McNeal.* "You seem… smarter."

"Oh, that?" she said, shrugging him off. "It's no great mystery. I'm wearing my editing outfit. I'm always smart when I wear this. Too bad you weren't leering. I have a slinky sequined dress that would be perfect for that. Want to see?"

Instantly, an image of Jessica Rabbit, the voluptuous redhead from the adult cartoon *Who Framed Roger Rabbit*, came to mind. The thought of Bunny wearing anything seductive made his stomach churn. "No!"

Gunter woofed his agreement.

Houdini answered with a bark from the second bedroom.

"Oh, poo, you're such a wet blanket," Bunny said sourly.

Okay, this nonsense had to stop before they woke the entire house. Jerry circled back around to the issue at hand. "Listen, I don't care how many downloads you get, you are not to write articles about my family."

"You can't do that." Bunny looked at Granny. "Tell him he can't do that."

"I'm afraid it's his choice," Granny said softly.

"But," Bunny began.

"His choice," Granny repeated.

It bothered him that his grandmother hadn't instantly agreed with him. "I forbid it."

Bunny pulled a notebook from her breast pocket, flipped it open and dislodged the pencil from behind her ear. She looked at the notebook. "What about..."

Jerry cut her off. "Whatever it is, the answer is no."

Gunter yawned and gave him a look as if to say, *Big mistake.*

Jerry sighed. "You too, Gunter?"

Gunter lowered to the floor.

"Okay, it's your funeral." Bunny shoved the pencil behind her ear and faded from view.

Jerry glanced at his grandmother. "That was a joke, right? I wasn't trying to make her mad. I just want her to stop writing about us."

"You'll get your wish," Granny told him. "Is there anything else?"

Great, from the sound of things, Bunny wasn't the only one he'd upset. Jerry picked up the coffee cup and took a drink. Finding it cold, he went to the sink, poured it out, and then poured himself another cup. "I'm not going to say I'm sorry for protecting my family," he said, returning to the room. "I don't like all these spirits constantly hovering over April."

"They are spirits, Jer. It's literally what they're supposed to do."

Gunter answered with a soft growl as Jerry fought the urge to roll his eyes.

"April has shown her willingness to help and appears to have an abundance of time to devote to the task. She hasn't set parameters, and until she does, they will continue to come." Granny patted his hand once more. "Talk to her, Jerry. Remind her you've been doing this a lot longer than she has."

"Don't you think I've tried? We were supposed to leave for Punxsutawney two days ago. April is a giver, and these spirits keep pulling at her heartstrings."

Granny gave his hand a gentle squeeze. "Then perhaps we need to find a different way to tug at those heartstrings."

"Such as?"

"Leave that one to me." Granny gave his hand another squeeze, then disappeared.

Jerry looked at Gunter. "That all went well, don't you think?"

Gunter lowered his head to his paws without comment.

Chapter Two

Even with Granny's promise to help, the morning proved to be a flurry of paranormal activity with spirits lining up to seek April's help. Unwilling to leave his future family unprotected, Jerry stayed close, leaving them to their tasks and only intervening when a spirit overstayed their welcome or otherwise proved obnoxious. That April seemed so at ease in her new role continued to amaze him and further let him know they were destined to be together. While he knew this was only the beginning of April's psychic abilities, he was glad she was able to start slowly, and further thankful she could not yet see the enormity of the task set before her.

April no sooner ended her conversation with one spirit than the spirit of a middle-aged man in a dark gray suit approached. Appearing to size her up, he stood in front of her without speaking for several seconds before extending his hand to her.

Jerry opened his mouth to tell the spirit to keep his hands to himself.

Too late. Both Gunter and Houdini positioned themselves between April and the handsy spirit, snarling their objections.

April glanced at Max, who was sitting next to her, drawing on her sketchpad. "What's going on?"

"The dogs don't seem to like him, but I think it's just because he got too close. I don't think he's anything to worry about, as I don't get a bad feeling from him," Max said reassuringly.

The spirit faded in and out.

"It's nothing to worry about," Jerry agreed. "Gunter and Houdini are just doing their job."

The spirit fully materialized and ran his hand through what was left of his hair.

Jerry stepped up beside April and eyed the spirit. "Unless you want to see what those dogs are capable of, I'd suggest you keep your hands to yourself."

The spirit shoved his hands in his pockets. "I…I didn't mean anything by it. I was just making sure I had the young lady's attention."

"You have it." The words had no sooner left Jerry's mouth than his cell rang, announcing Fred's call. "It's Fred. I'll be on the other side of the wall if you need anything."

April smiled. "I'm fine. Answer it before he

sends out a search party."

Though he knew she was kidding, when it came to Fred, it was a real possibility. Jerry swiped to answer the call as he left the room. "What's up, Boss?"

"McNeal, I could ask you the same thing. I thought you'd be in Chambersburg by now."

"The wedding was called off. June needed a minute to recover, so we decided to take our time getting there. We liked DuBois so much, we decided to stay for a bit longer." Okay, not exactly the truth, but the option was to tell him they'd remained in town so that April could hone her newfound gift. While Fred would find out eventually, April didn't need the added pressure of Fred recruiting her to do company business.

"Who got cold feet, the bride or the groom?"

"Neither; they decided to forgo the wedding altogether and elope."

Fred chuckled. "McNeal, I don't know whether to be proud or disappointed in you."

Jerry frowned. "How's that?"

"You've already popped the question, and there you had the perfect venue with everything already bought and paid for within a couple of hours' drive, and you didn't seize the day."

Jerry laughed. "Yeah, April's already balking at having a big wedding. Somehow I don't think I would have helped matters much by asking her to step into another bride's shadow."

"Probably not. How come April doesn't want all the pomp and circumstance?"

"She doesn't have any family."

"Of course, she does – our family. Tell her to name the place and time, and I'll walk her down the aisle myself."

Jerry smiled. "I'm sure that will make her feel better. Still, she says that with the exception of Carrie, the only friends she has were my friends first. She's worried about the chairs on the bride's side being empty."

"Can't you just have some of your friends sit on the other side?"

"Now you're just being logical," Jerry replied.

Fred chuckled. "Imagine that. Listen, I received a call from Sinclair."

"Is he still trying to get me to certify my other dog?"

"He pushed real hard, reminding me of the liability of such things."

"And you said?"

"Exactly what you told me to. I read him in on Gunter and what you do."

Jerry recalled his previous conversation of telling Sinclair about Gunter being a spirit. While the man hadn't believed him, something had resonated when he'd told Sinclair his daughter could see the dog. Jerry knew there was more to it than simple disbelief – a feeling further demonstrated by how fast the man had left the building. "What'd he say?"

"Nothing at first. He called back a few hours later and asked if I could send you his way. My gut tells me his wanting to see you doesn't come as a surprise."

"Nope."

"Care to elaborate?"

"Just a feeling I got when I met the man," Jerry said, omitting the part about Sinclair's daughter seeing spirits. Fred Jefferies seemed to be an alright fellow, but Jerry was still unsettled about his boss's intense need to surround himself with individuals who had psychic abilities. "Where does Sinclair live?"

"Florida. A couple of hours from The Villages. I figure it would give you a reason to visit your parents. Maybe tell them about your engagement in person."

Jerry raised an eyebrow. "And just how do you know I haven't told them yet?"

"It's my job to know these things." Fred laughed a hearty laugh. "Relax, McNeal, I'm not monitoring your calls. I know you well enough to know that you've been holding off telling them until you had something solid to tell. The fact that April already has cold feet can't help you feel all gooey about tying the knot."

"She doesn't have cold feet," Jerry replied.

"Maybe not, but she's not rushing toward that altar either."

Jerry stepped into the door frame, watching April speak with a spirit she couldn't see. "We'll get there," he said, meaning it.

"Good, then, a trip to Florida to give your parents the news seems to be in order."

"Did Sinclair give you an idea of the urgency of the matter?" Jerry spoke loud enough for April to hear then lowered his voice.

"The man tried to keep the conversation casual, but I detected a subtle sense of urgency in his voice. I know you had plans, but…"

"Don't worry about it, Boss; April and Max know that company business takes precedence over sightseeing. We'll wrap things up here and be on our way."

Fred chuckled once more. "Make sure to call your mom to let her know you're coming. You showing up unannounced is one thing – showing up unannounced with April and Max would be a major no-no."

Jerry recalled the last time he'd shown up without calling. "I'll give her a call."

"It's a long drive to Florida. Want me to send the jet?" Fred asked.

"No, we're good. April and I can switch off driving. I'll plan on meeting with him at the end of the week unless you need me there sooner." Jerry didn't bother to tell Fred he'd let him know when they left, as Fred would know.

"The end of the week is good. I'll send you the information. Make sure you call your mom. If not, you'll both get a surprise."

"What's that supposed to mean?"

"You're the psychic; figure it out."

"Or you could just stop playing games and tell me what you know."

Fred chuckled. "What I know is your parents moved."

"Moved? They would have told me if they left The Villages."

"They didn't leave The Villages. They moved to a different location."

"Huh, wonder why they didn't mention it?"

"Probably because you don't call them enough," Fred said and disconnected the call.

"What'd Fred want?" April asked when he entered the room.

"To tell me my parents moved."

"They moved and didn't tell you?"

"Apparently."

"How does Fred know?"

Jerry cocked an eyebrow.

April snickered. "Your parents move, and Fred has to be the first to drop the secret?"

"Naw, it just came up in conversation. Fred

called for company business," Jerry said, not wishing to say more around the spirits that filled the room.

A frown flitted across her face. "You're leaving?"

"We're leaving." Jerry looked over the line of spirits still waiting their turn. "After we wrap things up here."

Instantly, Bunny appeared. Dressed in a top hat and waistcoat with tails, she moved through the room, talking into a megaphone. "Okay, you heard what the man said. There's work to be done, so everyone clear out!"

Max giggled.

April frowned. "I don't know what you find so amusing. I wasn't finished talking to Mr. Bigsby yet."

Jerry moved up beside April and lowered his voice. "Max isn't laughing at what Bunny is saying. It's how she's going about it."

"Which is?" April asked.

"She looks like a circus barker," Jerry told her.

"That explains why her voice is so loud." April looked about the room. "I would have liked to have finished my conversation with Mr. Bigsby. I think his wife's in trouble."

Jerry frowned. "What kind of trouble?"

April sighed. "I can't be sure, but I think she's being catfished."

"Catfished."

"Scammed," April clarified.

"Unfortunately, it happens a lot," Jerry told her.

"What happens?"

"People preying on widows and widowers." Jerry offered April a hand. As he helped her from the couch, he wrapped his arms around her. "I understand wanting to help them all, but you won't always be able to."

"How do you deal with disappointing them?"

"It's not always easy. We do what we can and move on." He used his thumb to rub the crease between her eyebrows. "Just remember, you don't have to tackle this alone. We're a team, remember?"

"I remember." She stretched, gave him a quick kiss, then looked about the room. "Are they all gone?"

Jerry nodded. "They are."

April sighed and began gathering their stuff. "Max, you can finish that on the road. Go get your things together."

"Are we going to Florida with you?" Max asked as she closed her notebook.

April glanced at Jerry. "Florida?"

"It's where the job is."

"Do we get to go?" Max asked once more.

Jerry looked at April and smiled a sheepish smile. "My parents have been dying to meet you both."

"Jerry and I will talk about it," April promised.

Max left the room with Houdini on her heels.

"What's wrong with Gunter?" April asked when the dog woofed.

Jerry looked over at the dog, laughing out loud when Gunter licked his lips. "He seems to be excited about the Florida trip."

"He likes your parents?"

"Dad found out Gunter likes sweets and made a point of telling just about everyone in The Villages. Every time I turned around, someone was bringing a plate of desserts in hopes of getting a glimpse of the infamous ghost dog." Jerry moved close to April and lowered his voice to a whisper. "It's a good thing Gunter is a ghost, or he'd have left there weighing four hundred pounds."

April giggled when Gunter groaned. "Did he ever let anyone see him?"

"Nope, but a few got to see their treats disappear. Listen, I'm not trying to pressure you into going. If you'd prefer to go home, Fred will send the jet. But if you want to go, you and Max are welcome to come."

"Max has been looking forward to meeting them."

Jerry stepped closer and pulled her into his arms. "They are going to love you both."

"And if they don't?"

"They will."

"How can you be so sure?"

"I'm psychic, remember?" Jerry winked. "Stop worrying. All they are going to see is how happy you make me. Isn't that what all parents want for their children?"

April lowered her eyes. "Most parents."

Jerry lifted April's chin and kissed her.

"What was that for?"

"I can't take away your past, but I can promise you a future full of love."

April sighed. "If I had to endure the past to get to where I am now, it was well worth it."

Gunter groaned.

April giggled. "Gunter doesn't like sappy?"

Jerry pulled her closer. "I'm pretty sure that was his way of telling us to get a room, and while I agree with the sentiment, we really do need to get going."

Chapter Three

Having loaded the Durango, Jerry stood in the kitchen looking over the instructions for checking out. A male voice in the front room drew his attention. He returned to the living room and saw April speaking with the spirit she'd been talking with previously. While she looked calm, both Gunter and Houdini stood between her and the spirit.

"What's going on?" Jerry asked casually.

April jumped at the sound of his voice.

Jerry looked at Mr. Bigsby. "Did the lady invite you, or did you just return on your own?"

"We had unfinished business," he said without apology.

"Then I take it she didn't invite you."

April shook her head.

"Leave," Jerry said firmly.

The spirit balked. "But I—"

Both Gunter and Houdini bared their fangs.

"You'd rather deal with them?" Jerry asked, motioning to the dogs.

Bigsby disappeared.

"He's gone," Jerry told her as both Gunter and Houdini stood down.

Gunter sat lazily scratching an imaginary itch while Houdini sidled up to April, seeking her praise for scaring off the unwanted spirit.

April ran her hands through the young dog's fur. "Yes, you're a good boy." She looked at Jerry. "I'm sorry."

"You have nothing to apologize for."

"Maybe I made him come back. I was thinking about him. Maybe he felt it," she said softly. "I'm sorry. I didn't mean to make you mad."

Jerry felt his jaw twitch, and he worked to keep his voice even. "I'm not your ex. You don't owe me an apology. I'm not mad, April. I just want you to know how important it is to set boundaries. Those who've crossed over don't need rest. They don't need to sleep or worry about their mental health. Doing what we do can take a physical toll on both our minds and our bodies. It is important to protect yourself."

"You don't have to worry about me."

Though she looked at Houdini when she spoke, Jerry knew her words were directed at him. "It's literally my job to worry about you."

"I know. I'm just not used to having people fuss over me."

"You'd better get used to it because I don't intend to stop."

"Okay, but full confession, while I know it's irrational, a part of me thinks I should stay here and finish what I started."

"The only irrational thing is thinking you'll ever finish this. Remember that baseball movie with the tagline 'If you build it, they will come'?"

April batted her eyes at him. "*Field of Dreams*?"

"That's the one. It's the same. The spirits know what you can do, so they will find you."

April's eyes brightened. "Even Mr. Bigsby?"

Jerry nodded. "Even Mr. Bigsby, which is why I am serious about you setting boundaries. If you allow them to, they will invade your every waking moment. I'm talking twenty-four-seven."

April smiled her understanding. "You speak from experience."

Jerry fought to keep the memories of his early years dealing with spirits at bay. "Have you seen those videos where the baby gets a hearing aid and is able to hear for the first time, or glasses, and is able to see when all they've known is darkness?"

She nodded. "I have."

"It's like that with the spirits. They know what you can do and will invade all your senses until there's barely anything left for anything else."

"Are you worried there won't be enough left for you?" April asked softly.

Yes. He worked to tone down his fears. "Maybe."

She smiled a reassuring smile. "You're not going to get rid of me that easy."

"Good, 'cause I'd hate to play the neanderthal card."

"Which is?"

"Throwing you over my shoulder and dragging you from the house kicking and screaming."

April giggled a nervous giggle. "You wouldn't dare."

Always up for a challenge, Jerry took a step.

April's giggles turned into a playful gasp as she pulled Houdini in front of her for protection. Houdini considered this a fun new game and squirmed to slather her with doggie kisses.

Gunter joined in, dipping into a playful bow while barking his encouragement.

"No fair," April said, backing her way up the back of the couch. "It's three against one."

"All's fair in love and war," Jerry said, moving closer.

Gunter's barks morphed into a soulful howl.

April attempted to shush the dog. "Gunter, stop. Max will hear."

Houdini joined in on the ghostly chorus as a series of loud beeps filled the air.

April gazed at her phone, which sat on the table. "It sounds like an Amber alert."

It did, only his phone never alerted. He pulled his cell phone from his pocket and checked the screen. *Nothing.* "Easy, boys," Jerry said, reaching for April's phone and handing it to her.

She sat on the back of the couch and read the screen. "I was right; it's an Amber alert—Phillip King. He's four years old, with brown hair and brown eyes."

"Where?" Jerry asked.

"Punxsutawney."

"That's not too far from here."

Max hurried into the room. Her eyes were bright as she held her phone for them to see. "Did you get it?"

Jerry frowned. "No. But your mom did."

"We need to go! You said it's not that far. Houdini can find him, I know he can." Max looked from him to her mother. "Mom, why are you on the back of the couch?"

"Spider," April said without missing a beat. "Big scary one. Didn't you hear the dogs barking?"

Max shrugged. "Nope. I had my headphones in, looking at videos, when the alert came in."

"Good." April stood, balancing on the couch.

Max blinked her confusion. "Huh?"

"It's good the Amber alert overrode the videos," April replied.

Jerry had to hand it to her, the woman was quick. He moved closer to help her down. "You're good," he whispered.

She rewarded him with a smile. "And you're bad."

"Eww." Max wrinkled her nose.

"At killing spiders," April said, expanding her sentence.

Granny appeared at Max's side. "Come along, dear; Jerry has to take a phone call."

The words had no sooner been uttered than Jerry's cell rang, alerting him to Fred's call.

April's eyes grew wide. "Wow, she's good."

Too good. Jerry waited until Max went outside then swiped to answer the call. "Hello."

"There's an Amber alert in your area." Fred's words were full of static.

Okay, first, Jerry hadn't gotten the alert, and now his signal was questionable. He'd not had problems with cell phone reception in years. As a matter of fact, his reception was so good at times that he jokingly thought of it as being tapped into the angel network. Jerry moved around the room, trying to get reception. "Are you there?"

"I'm here, I said. It seems a bit odd that the alert didn't come through regular channels. Even so, I think it would be a good chance to see what that pup of yours can do."

Instantly, Jerry recalled his grandmother's

promise to find a way to pull at April's heartstrings. The hairs on the back of his neck tingled. Surely his grandmother hadn't been involved in the child's disappearance. "Hang on a sec, I'll let April and Max know." Jerry walked back to the living room. "April, let Max know she's getting her wish. We've been called into action."

April's face lit up. "We get to help look for the little boy?"

Jerry nodded and walked to the kitchen, searching for a better signal. Finding one, he spoke into the phone. "What do you mean when you say the alert didn't go through regular channels?"

"Just what I said. We didn't get the alert on our end. The tech guy caught it when it was delivered to April's and Max's phones. Odd that it didn't go to yours. Maybe you should try to reboot."

Okay, that made sense. It had been a while since doing so. Still, something about the alert bugged him, and he was about to ask if his boss found it suspicious when Fred next spoke.

"You know how critical the timing is on these things. I authorize you to use your lights and siren if necessary."

Jerry beamed his good fortune; not only had his grandmother found a way to take April's mind off the spirits, but knowing how much he loved a good chase, she'd given him something to boot. *Betty Lou, you beautiful old soul, remind me to hug you when I see you.* "Lights and sirens. Roger, that, sir."

"I thought you might like that. Do try to keep it under a hundred."

Jerry laughed. "Have you seen the stretch of road between here and Punxsutawney? It's like a coiled snake threw up a highway – some stretches are no better than driving in a slinky."

"Keep talking like that, and I'll revoke your speeding privileges."

"Relax, Boss; I've driven that stretch enough to know my limits."

"Okay, McNeal, keep me apprised of the situation."

The phone grew silent. Jerry studied it, wondering if Fred actually ended their conversation or if the call had been dropped. He toggled the buttons to restart the phone and waited for it to come back online. "Two bars, that's odd."

Gunter yawned.

"Everything okay?" April asked, coming into the room.

Jerry shoved his phone into his pocket. "I'm good, but I'm not so sure about my phone."

"Did you try rebooting it?"

"Just did."

"And?"

"And we'll see."

"How long have you had it?"

"I don't know. It's been a few years."

April laughed. "Two years is considered a dinosaur."

Jerry frowned. "It was working fine until today."

"Don't look so worried. We can always get you a new phone," April told him.

Jerry took her hand in his and kissed her engagement ring. "You're right. It's only a phone," he said, leaving out the fact that he felt there was much more to it than simply replacing the device. As he followed her outside, he couldn't get past the feeling that something was terribly wrong.

The feeling of unease continued when he reached the Durango and saw Max sitting in the backseat with Houdini. While perfectly normal, they'd always traveled with a spiritual entourage. Not seeing any gave him a feeling of being totally and utterly alone. Jerry pushed the thought aside as Gunter appeared in the backseat beside them. *Relax, McNeal. You'd be complaining if the seats were full.* While the little pep talk helped, Jerry took a moment to walk around the Durango, kicking each tire as he went.

"Are you sure you're okay?" April asked when he slid behind the wheel.

"Just double-checking everything before we go." Jerry started the SUV. As he pulled out of the driveway, he turned on the lights and siren.

"This is so exciting!" April said as Jerry slowed for a red light then continued when ensuring traffic stopped.

"It's also dangerous," Jerry reminded her.

"What do you want us to do?"

Jerry maneuvered around a car that pulled to the side while staying mostly on the road. "Nothing. Don't try to help. If I stop at an intersection, lean back in your seat. I don't want to have to look around you to see. It's not that I don't trust you, but I'm the driver. If anything happens, it is on me."

"Got it. You want us to pretend we aren't here."

"Just until we get to where we're going." He glanced in the rearview mirror to gauge Max's reaction. Not only didn't she look at him, he couldn't pick up on anything. Yes, something was definitely wrong. He gripped the wheel and focused on the road. While things felt off, he still had a job to do.

Once outside city limits, Jerry's training took over, and he settled into the drive, watching the road and surroundings and looking for threats. The Durango's power felt good, and he'd driven it so much, he knew what it was capable of. He'd missed this. He turned on the radio and hit the button for his preloaded list.

"This isn't Joe Bonamassa," April mused.

Jerry grinned. "Nope. There's traveling music and there's music that will get you in the zone. The song's called 'Bootleg Turn' by Justin Johnson. He's the guy I showed you on YouTube who plays the shovel." They passed a line of cars pulled to the shoulder, then veered right onto US 119 S.

A car started to pull out of a side street. Jerry slowed, then increased his speed when the car yielded. As he drove, he focused on the little boy, trying to get a reading, and wished they'd put a photo with the name. If someone had taken the child, he didn't want to take any chances of passing them along the way. *Where are you, Phillip King?*

Nothing.

It wasn't the music; he often listened to tunes when he drove. Nor did he think it had to do with the fact that he had April and Max with him. Not only couldn't he get a reading on the boy, he couldn't get a reading period. Almost as if the gift had left him. No, that wasn't true. His feelings were pegging in all directions, telling him something was wrong.

There were multiple small towns along the way. While Jerry continued to run with lights and sirens, he lowered the music and slowed his speed considerably each time they passed through the rural neighborhoods where the houses were set right next to the road. He drove through Big Run 15 above the 35 MPH speed limit, his gaze darting from side to side, watching for threats. Making it through the town without issue, he pressed the pedal to increase his speed. As the needle crept up, his neck tingled.

"Jerry!" both April and Max yelled at the same time.

A large black dog raced from the porch of a

house to the right, followed by a tow-haired boy who looked to be no older than four or five. Though there were several children playing in the yard, it was apparent the dog was headed to the road. The boy followed.

Jerry pressed his foot against the pedal. As the duo reached the street, the Durango's warning system kicked in, sounding an alarm. The SUV came to a halt as the dog disappeared into the stand of trees on the opposite side of the road. He held his breath, waiting for the boy to follow.

Nothing.

Unwilling to face the carnage he'd caused, Jerry gripped the wheel. *God, please don't let him be dead.*

Several kids stood peeking above the hedges as a woman raced from the house. Her screams filled the air as she ran into the road and disappeared in front of the SUV.

"Did we hit him?" April's voice was barely above a whisper.

Jerry looked in the mirror to gauge Max's reaction. To his dismay, the girl offered no clues.

Jerry's heart caught in his throat as his mind took in the gravity of the situation. With a stand of trees to the left of the road and the children standing in the yard, had April and Max not alerted him, someone would have been killed. "Stay here!"

Jerry turned off the siren but left the lights on as he got out. He took a breath as he walked to the front, letting it out as he saw the child standing in his mother's embrace. While the boy was crying, he did not appear to have a scratch on him. He gave April a thumbs-up to let her know the child was okay. As he did, his fear morphed into anger. "What were you thinking running into the street like that?! Didn't you hear the siren?!"

Instead of reacting, the boy continued to cry. Looking toward the woods, he used his hands to ask his mother about the dog.

Jerry swallowed his understanding and amended his tone. "The boy's deaf?"

The woman nodded through tear-filled eyes. "It's my fault. Jasper's been watching squirrels all morning. I should have known he would bolt the moment Tommy opened the door. I had my reservations about getting a dog with the house sitting so close to the street. I've always been afraid of the dog getting hit by a car. I never dreamed I could have lost my son the same way."

"Not this time, but you do need to get the situation under control." The words were no sooner spoken than Gunter broke through the trees followed closely by the lab. The lab stopped to sniff the child before following Gunter to the porch. Jerry watched as a car eased past them, the driver craning his neck to see what was going on. "Best get you both out of the street. Is Jasper your son's service dog?"

"He's Tommy's dog, but he's not a service dog.

We're on the list to get one, but I guess those things take time. My husband insisted we get a lab, saying he would help protect him. What he did is nearly get him killed." She narrowed her eyes as Tommy bent and wrapped his arms around the dog.

"It's not the dog's fault. He was only doing what dogs do. I have a few connections. Give me your contact information, and I'll see if I can help." Jerry pulled out his pad to draw the woman's attention as Tommy reached a hand to pet Gunter, who'd moved up next to the boy as he fawned over the lab.

"Mary Shepherd," she said, then rattled off the rest of her contact information. "I know you were in a hurry. I'm sorry for keeping you."

Jerry thought about Phillip King and realized he would be around the same age as Tommy. He then hoped that case would have the same outcome. "We're going to help look for a little boy about your son's age. As you know, they can get away from you pretty quickly."

"I'll do better," Mary said more to herself than to him.

Chapter Four

"You said the boy is okay, but how about you, are you alright?" April asked when he returned to the Durango.

"I'll do." Jerry knew it wasn't an answer, but it was the only one he had. He placed the SUV in drive but decided to forgo the siren since they were close to Punxsutawney. That and going fast had momentarily lost its draw.

"Fred called," April said after a moment. "I guess they got an alert about the hard brake and saw we were stopped and wanted to make sure everything was okay. He said he tried to call your phone, but you didn't answer."

Jerry leaned to the left, pulled his phone from his pocket, and handed it to April. "Check for a call."

April frowned. "I don't see any missed calls."

"That's because the phone isn't working."

April placed it in the cup holder and put her hand on his arm. "It's okay, Jerry. Fred remote-checked the camera while you were out. He said that was some outstanding driving, and that little boy was lucky you have the gift. He said if anyone else had been driving, it would probably have been a different outcome. He's right. That little boy is alive because of you."

"He could have just as easily been dead because of me," Jerry snapped.

April removed her hand.

Jerry sighed and reached for it once more. Bringing the hand to his lips, he kissed it just above the ring before releasing it. "I'm sorry. We're almost there. I don't want to chance any more close calls."

"Of course," she said softly.

Jerry glanced in the mirror, saw Max watching, and tried unsuccessfully to get a read on her thoughts. *What am I missing?* If Max heard the question, she didn't acknowledge it. He drummed his fingers on the steering wheel, replaying the moments before he stopped. While his intuition had been on alert, it hadn't pinged enough for him to react. That had come after April and Max called his name. Jerry's jaw twitched as he replayed the scene once more. Both of them had called his name before either the dog or the boy ran outside. Max, he could understand; her abilities were more fine-tuned than his, but why April? Could it be her gift was evolving? While he didn't doubt it would happen, he didn't think that was the case, as she would have said something. It didn't add up.

Jerry glanced in the mirror. Max saw him looking and turned toward the window. Jerry returned his attention to the road. Given Max's scowl and the fact she wouldn't make eye contact, he knew that he'd been right. Max was keeping something from him. Instead of upsetting him, it eased his mind knowing that even though something was off, his intuition was still on point.

The moment they came into the heart of the town, Max's sour mood vanished. "There's a groundhog!" she squealed when the first of the groundhog statues came into view.

Jerry looked to see a five-foot groundhog holding an umbrella that read "Save for a rainy day." The statue sat in a bank parking lot and the belly gave the impression of being a bank.

April picked up her phone to capture a picture.

"There will be time for photos later," Jerry promised. "First, we need to see about the boy."

"Of course," April said, lowering the phone. "Where are the cops? I mean, if they are looking for the boy, shouldn't we have seen some by now?"

It was a good point and one he'd already been mulling over, not having seen any checkpoints when coming into town. If someone had taken the child, they could be long gone by now. Then again, perhaps the local law enforcement knew something he did not and was trying to keep the search low key.

"What are you doing?" April asked when Jerry turned off the blue lights.

"Something is off."

"What something?"

"I wish I knew."

April giggled a nervous giggle. "That's reassuring. Nothing coming up on your spidey senses?"

"I'm only getting enough to tell me something is off."

April turned and looked over her seat. "What about you, Max? Are you picking anything up?"

"No."

Though April didn't seem to notice, Jerry could tell the word was forced.

"There's a police officer!" April said, pulling his attention from Max.

Jerry's internal radar dinged when he looked to see not one, but three police officers standing talking to a group of men dressed in formal attire. He spotted a parking spot and pulled to the curb.

Max got out without waiting to be told and motioned Houdini to her side. Gunter appeared beside the vehicle, only instead of joining Jerry, he sidled up to April instead. Ordinarily, Jerry would take this as a sign that April was in imminent danger, but none of his senses were alerting him to that. No, this felt more personal somehow.

As if reading his mind, Gunter smiled a K-9 smile and looked at him as if to say, *Get over yourself, McNeal. This isn't a popularity contest.*

The dog was right. He had a job to do and was wasting time trying to figure out what was wrong. He needed to focus on the boy and worry about the rest later. Moving into cop mode, he surveyed the park. "Max?"

"Yes."

"If Houdini is working, he needs to wear his vest." He handed April the keys to the Durango. "It's on top of the suitcases in the back. I'm going to go see what's going on."

One of the officers broke rank and walked to meet him as he approached. A tall fellow with a no-nonsense scowl, he looked Jerry over. "Can I help you?"

"My name is Jerry McNeal. My fiancée April and her daughter Max are with me. We were hoping to help you with your search," Jerry said with a nod to Max and April, who had just arrived with Houdini. Now wearing his vest, Houdini stood tall, ears alert as his nose sniffed the air. "Max is the dog's handler. Among other things, he is a certified SARs dog."

The officer's face remained noncommittal. "Who told you about the search?"

That the man hadn't said no let Jerry know the boy hadn't been found. That the men were standing around instead of looking for the child led him to believe they'd never organized a search before. Hoping to get things moving, Jerry decided to play his hand. "It went out over the wire. We were in the area, so the agency sent us here to help."

This got the officer's attention as he raised an eyebrow. "What agency?"

"The one who prefers not to be named, Officer Wagner," Jerry replied, using the name on the man's uniform.

"And they'd bring you in on something like this?"

"As I said, we were in the area, and the dog is highly trained. Do you by chance have a piece of clothing or something with Phillip's scent on it?"

Wagner frowned. "You're kidding, right?"

Tired of wasting precious time, Jerry stepped around the officer and into the clutch of men. "Who's in charge here?"

Officer Wagner pointed his thumb in Jerry's direction. "He said the F.B.I. sent him to help us find Phil."

Jerry shook his head. "I never said I was with the F.B.I. I said 'agency.'"

"What's the difference?" a man in a topcoat and tails asked.

Jerry smiled. "We outrank them."

The man eyed Max. "You're saying the girl works for this agency?"

"We all do," Jerry said, knowing it was only a matter of time before Fred brought April into the fold. "Mr. Mayor, I don't know if you are aware of the statistics, but the first twenty-four hours are critical in the search."

The mayor looked him up and down. "You know who I am?"

"The top hat kind of gave it away," Jerry told him. "Sir, if I may be bold, you sent that Amber alert out ninety minutes ago. We need to get to work organizing a search party, and we need to start now."

The group of men closed ranks.

The mayor worried his fingers around the brim of his hat. "That, young man, is precisely what has me perplexed. We did not send out an Amber alert. We sent out a coded message to a small team who is specially trained in such things so as not to alert the town and cause a public uproar."

"If you'll excuse me from saying so, a public uproar is exactly what you need. Plus, you need to set up roadblocks at the edge of town. No one out unless their vehicle is searched," Jerry said firmly.

April touched his arm and nodded toward Max, who was walking across the lawn following Houdini's lead. "I'm going with Max."

Glad to see someone was taking the search seriously, Jerry nodded his agreement.

Another man spoke up, drawing his attention. "We'll accept your help searching the square, but I doubt the roadblocks will be necessary. It's close to lunchtime. I doubt he has ventured much further than the square."

The mayor nodded his agreement. "Good point, Shackelford. We'll bring in the team and narrow our search."

"Team? You mean you already have people looking for him?"

The mayor bobbed his head. "Of course. They started the moment the alert went out. I told you we take our job as caretakers seriously. Just because we've never had a security breach of this kind doesn't mean we haven't trained for it."

Okay, that was a bit of a relief. "What about his parents? Did they have anything to say?"

Officer Wagner snickered.

The mayor furrowed his brow. "Say?"

"Yes, have you spoken with them? Perhaps they could give some insight about where their son has gone."

The mayor spoke up. "Who did you say you worked for?"

"He didn't," Wagner said, speaking for him.

Jerry's spidey senses tingled. "I told you I work for the agency."

"Prove it."

Jerry realized he'd failed to return his wallet to

his pocket after getting gas. "I'm the Lead Paranormal Investigator with the Department of Defense. My badge is in the Durango, but I don't have the keys with me."

Shackelford looked at Wagner. "Lead Paranormal Investigator. Is that even a thing?"

Wagner chuckled. "Far as I know, the government doesn't hire ghostbusters. Though he did have police lights when he rolled up."

"Isn't impersonating a police officer a crime?" one of the other men asked.

Wagner smiled.

Jerry looked at Gunter, who'd remained behind and now stood watching the proceedings. *Hello, dog. A little help here if you don't mind.*

Instead of springing into action, Gunter sat on his haunches, scratching an imaginary itch.

A dream. That's it. This is all a crazy dream.

Wagner stepped around him and slapped a cuff on his right wrist.

Funny, it doesn't feel like a dream. He thought about pulling his hand away but didn't want to add resisting arrest to whatever charge they were planning to stick him with. Instead, he concentrated on Max. *Kiddo, if you can hear me, tell your mom to call Fred and get this straightened out.*

April and Max appeared around the corner as Wagner led him to the police car. The look of shocked disbelief on April's face at seeing him being led away in cuffs was like a punch in the gut.

"That's enough!" Max yelled as Wagner helped him into the back of the cruiser. Only, as her words floated through the air, Jerry knew they were intended for someone he couldn't see.

Chapter Five

Earlier that day…

Granny materialized before her and sat on the edge of the bed, patting the spot beside her. "Maxine, I need to speak with you."

That Granny had appeared unexpectedly didn't scare her. That she'd used her given name and sounded serious terrified her. Max sat and pivoted to face the spirit. "What's wrong?"

Granny smiled. "You don't miss a thing, do you, child?"

"I try not to."

"You do a fine job. You'll go far in life as long as you remember you can't do everything on your own. It's okay to want to be independent, but there comes a time when you need to push pride aside and allow others to help you."

"You're talking about Jerry, aren't you?" Max asked.

"Like I said, you're a smart girl." A sadness touched the spirit's eyes. "Jerry has decided he doesn't need our help."

"Jerry loves you," Max replied.

"I know, but he thinks he can do what he does on his own, so we need to honor his wishes."

"He didn't mean it. I know he didn't," Max insisted.

"Maybe not, but until he recants his order to leave him alone, we are not able to help."

"Then I'll let him know so he can fix it."

"No, child. You mustn't interfere. Jerry's a grown man; he needs to learn the consequences of his request."

The image of a little boy flashed in Max's mind and a cold chill raced down her spine as a great foreboding engulfed her. "We won't be able to find the boy, will we?"

"Things aren't always as they seem, Maxine."

"Then why am I scared?"

"You will be there to protect him," Granny promised.

"Protect Jerry or the boy?"

Granny smiled. "Protecting one will protect the other."

"How will I know?" Max swallowed her fear. "I'm sorry, I know you don't always like telling us things. I just don't want to let Jerry down."

"Stop worrying, child. I will be there when you need me." Granny glanced at the door when April called for Max. "You feel me with you, don't you?"

Max nodded.

"That's because you've accepted my help."

Suddenly, what the woman was saying became clear. "Jerry won't be able to feel you, will he?"

Granny shook her head. "Not until he learns his lesson."

Fear engulfed her. "But what if he doesn't learn his lesson?"

"Jerry's a smart man." Granny placed her palm on Max's cheek. "You mustn't tell him. It's important he figures it out on his own."

While Max wanted to believe her, she still felt unsettled at keeping things from Jerry. "You're right, he is smart. He'll ask me what is going on and know if I'm lying to him."

Granny removed her hand. "I'm not asking you to lie to him."

"But he'll ask."

"Then tell him you don't know."

"But—"

"It's okay, Maxine. I have not told you of our plan. You cannot tell what you do not know, and Jerry cannot glean from you what you do not wish him to hear. Do you understand?"

Understanding the request, Max nodded once

more. "You want me to block him from my thoughts."

"Fret not, my dear. It is for Jerry's own good."

Max knew Granny loved Jerry and wouldn't do anything to purposely harm him. "Okay, Granny."

"You're a good girl, Max."

"Granny?"

"Yes, Max?"

"Will it take long for Jerry to learn his lesson?"

The spirit smiled once more. "It will take as long as it takes."

That wasn't good enough. "I love Jerry. I don't want him to think I'm mad at him, nor do I want him mad at me."

Her mother's giggles filled the air.

Granny's eyes twinkled. "I'll see what I can do to speed up the process."

"Thanks, Granny. You're the best."

"Make sure you remember that when things feel a little bleak."

Before Max could answer, a shrill tone pierced the air. Max looked at her cell phone and saw it was an Amber alert. As she silenced her phone, Gunter howled, drowning out the laughter. Seconds later, Houdini joined him in a ghostly chorus.

Max read the alert for a missing four-year-old boy in Punxsutawney. "This is my chance to show them what Houdini can do!" Forgetting her earlier distress, she raced to the front room to beg Jerry to allow them to help with the search. To her surprise, her mother was sitting on the back of the couch. *Okay, that could explain the laughter.*

Max held up her phone, showing the alert. "Did you get it?"

Jerry shook his head. "No. But your mom did."

"We need to go! You said it's not that far. Houdini can find him. I know he can." The absurdity of her mother's predicament struck her. "Mom, why are you sitting on the back of the couch?"

"Spider," April said without missing a beat. "Big scary one. Didn't you hear the dogs barking?"

Not wanting to let on she hadn't heard anything because she was too busy talking to Granny, Max shrugged. "Nope. I had my headphones in looking at videos when the alert came in and they howled." She felt the heat of the lie and quickly blocked them both from learning the truth.

April stood, gingerly picking her way along the sofa. "Good."

Good? What kind of answer was that? "Huh?"

"It's good the Amber alert overrode the videos," April said.

Jerry moved closer to help her mother down. As he did, he whispered something Max couldn't hear.

Her mother smiled. "And you're bad."

Instantly, Max knew there'd been no spider. "Eww."

"At killing spiders," her mother said

unconvincingly.

Granny appeared at her side. "Come along, dear; Jerry has to take a phone call."

"Start packing," Granny whispered as Jerry's cell rang. "That's Mr. Fred calling to have Jerry take you and Houdini to help with the search."

"Yes!" Max whispered.

Several moments later, April knocked on her bedroom door and poked her head into the room. "Get your things together; we're going to help with the search."

"Already on it." Max shrugged. "Granny told me."

April smiled. "Hi, Granny."

"Hello, Granddaughter," Granny called in return.

April laughed. "Not yet."

"You will be," Granny told her.

April beamed her response and shut the door once more.

"It is important you remember our talk," Granny said as Max hoisted her backpack over her shoulder and grabbed the suitcase handle.

Max bobbed her head. "I remember." Though she was worried about Jerry, the thought of being involved in a real search had her giddy. Houdini fell in beside her as she made her way to the Durango where Granny was waiting for her when she arrived.

The excitement of helping with the search ebbed as Jerry looked through the SUV window and frowned. *He knows. Don't be paranoid; you blocked him, so he can't possibly know.* Max shook off the thought. Even still, something was troubling him; she could feel the anxiety radiating off him.

Granny placed a hand on her knee. "Let it play out, Maxine. This is Jerry's cross to bear, not yours. You'll not be doing him any favors by helping him."

"Yes, ma'am." Max bit her tongue as Jerry walked around the Durango as if looking for something he couldn't see. She could feel his unease as the energy vibrated, and she wanted nothing more than to break her silence and tell him what was wrong. It wasn't fair. While she loved Granny, her loyalty was to Jerry. The spirit must have known it as she sat beside her, resting her hand on Max's knee.

Max's heart began to race the moment Jerry turned on the siren, and the image of the little boy came to mind once more. Only this time, the child was running straight toward them. Max firmed her chin. Letting Jerry find his way was one thing, but Jerry was a good man. There was no way he'd be able to live with himself if he did something to harm anyone, much less an innocent boy. She blocked Granny from hearing her thoughts and focused on the road as Jerry turned on the radio.

Was that it? Was the radio so loud, Jerry would not be able to tap into his gift? Max watched as he settled into the seat, and noted how his energy calmed as he drove. She remembered the first time she'd ridden with him when they went looking for Ashley Fabel's body. He'd been focused much as he appeared to be now; only then, had it been because he was allowing Gunter to take the lead.

But you're not helping him now, are you, Gunter?

The ghostly K-9 answered by lowering his muzzle to her shoulder with a heavy sigh. Instantly, Max knew Granny must have forbidden him from helping as well. She started to tell Jerry he wasn't alone when Granny increased the pressure on her knee.

Jerry slowed as he drove through a town.

Max felt the energy strengthen. She leaned forward in the seat, watching for the boy. Instead of slowing, Jerry increased his speed. Max's heart began to race as her senses screamed that danger was near. Suddenly, she didn't care about letting him find his way; or what Granny would do if she didn't listen. *Jerry Stop!* "JERRY!"

"JERRY!" April screamed at the same time.

As the Durango slid to a stop, a flash of black caught her attention. Max realized the flash was a dog. The dog ran toward the street, followed closely by the same little blonde-haired boy she'd seen in her premonition. The dash beeped its warning as Max braced for an impact that never came.

Screams filled the air as a woman raced through

the yard and into the street and disappeared in front of the Durango.

"Did we hit them?" Her mother's voice was barely above a whisper.

Jerry looked in the mirror.

Afraid to move, Max tried to get a read on the kid, who had to be frightened. Only when she focused on the boy, she was met with silence. While she didn't think they'd hit the boy, she wondered why she couldn't pick up anything.

Jerry killed the siren. "Stay here!"

Houdini whined as Gunter followed him from the SUV.

Max held her breath as Jerry ducked in front of the car. A second later, he extended his thumb.

"That was a close one," Bunny said, appearing in the seat beside her.

"It had to be done," Granny whispered so April couldn't hear.

April blew a ragged breath between the palms of her hands. "Oh, thank God. I thought for sure we'd killed him. We would have if you hadn't told him to stop."

But I didn't. Max blinked her confusion. "I did?"

"Yes, right before we called his name."

Funny, she couldn't recall telling him to stop. "I can't hear him."

"You can't hear Jerry?"

"No, the boy. Jerry motioned that he was okay,

but I can't hear him."

April turned in her seat. "You mean he's dead."

"No. I can feel him. I just can't hear him." Max watched as Gunter disappeared into the stand of trees. "Gunter's going after the boy's dog."

"Good. Hopefully, he'll talk some sense into him." Her mother must have realized what she'd said as she giggled.

"It's not as crazy as you think," Max told her. "He schools Houdini all the time."

The dash lit up, announcing Fred's call.

April connected the call. "Hi, Fred, Jerry's busy."

"I know, our tech guy reviewed the camera when the alert came in. You tell that man of yours I said that was some outstanding driving. It's a good thing his gift alerted him to stop. That boy would have been dead if anyone else was driving."

"I'll let him know," April promised, then ended the call without telling Fred that it was she and Max who had alerted Jerry. April's voice trembled when she next spoke. "Is Jerry okay? He seems off."

Max struggled with how to respond. While Granny hadn't specifically told her not to tell her mom, she had the impression the woman wouldn't approve of her doing so. Max decided it best to evade the question. "He's just worried about the boy."

"I know, but I got the feeling something was wrong even before we got the alert. Shh, he's coming," April said at seeing Jerry return to the SUV. She waited for him to settle into the driver's seat, then directed the same question to him. "You said the boy is okay, but how about you, are you alright?"

"I'll do."

While he'd managed to sound convincing, Max knew he was lying. If her mother had picked up on it, she didn't let on.

"Fred called," her mother told him. "I guess they got an alert about the hard brake and wanted to make sure everything was okay. He said he tried to call your phone, but you didn't answer."

Jerry leaned to the left, pulled his phone from his pocket, and handed it to her mother. "Check for a call."

April shook her head. "I don't see any missed calls."

"That's because the phone isn't working."

April placed the phone in the cup holder and put her hand on his arm. "It's okay, Jerry. Fred remote-checked the camera while you were out. He said that was some outstanding driving, and that little boy was lucky you have the gift. He said if anyone else had been driving, it would probably have been a different outcome. That little boy is alive because of you."

"He could have just as easily been dead because of me," Jerry snapped.

Max's heart ached as her mother pulled her hand away.

No, I'll not let you destroy our family, Max said silently.

"Maxine," Granny whispered. "I know this is difficult for you, but I promise you it is for Jerry's own good."

"Your grandmother is right." Bunny's voice was just as quiet.

"You couldn't hear him because he is deaf," Granny told her.

Now the silence made sense as Max absorbed what she said.

Jerry reached for her mother's hand. "I'm sorry. We're almost there. I don't want to chance any more close calls."

"Of course."

Her mother's words were barely above a whisper. Max knew she was on the verge of crying.

She saw Jerry looking at her in the rearview mirror. *What am I missing?* he asked without speaking.

She continued her betrayal and blocked him from knowing he'd reached her. She turned toward the window so she didn't have to look into his eyes. She tried to concentrate on Phillip King but saw nothing. While the alert didn't have a photo, she should have gotten something by now, which led her to wonder if this was part of Jerry's test. The thought angered her, as she'd hoped to show everyone what Houdini could do. She caught a glimpse of blue and realized she was looking at one of the groundhog statues Jerry had told her about. Standing nearly as tall as she, it looked to be a bank. "There's a groundhog!"

"There will be time for photos later. First, we need to see about the boy," Jerry said when her mother attempted to take a photo.

"Of course." Her mother's voice was stronger now. "Where are the cops? I mean, if they are looking for the boy, shouldn't we have seen some by now?"

While Gunter sat quietly, Houdini practically vibrated with anticipation. Max wasn't sure if it was the unsettled energy inside the SUV or if he knew something she'd yet to figure out.

"What are you doing?" April asked, drawing her attention.

"Something is off," Jerry responded.

"What something?"

"I wish I knew."

April giggled a nervous giggle. "That's reassuring. Nothing coming up on your spidey senses?"

"I'm only getting enough to tell me something is off."

April looked over her seat. "What about you, Max? Are you picking anything up?"

"No," Max said truthfully.

April swiveled and pointed out the window. "There's a police officer!"

Jerry pulled to the curb.

Max got out and motioned Houdini to her side. Even though Max knew Gunter was just following orders, it still hurt to see him go to her mother instead of helping Jerry. She took comfort that the dog felt this situation to be temporary, for if not, he would have vanished altogether.

"If Houdini is working, he needs to wear his vest." Jerry handed the keys to April. "It's on top of the suitcases in the back. I'm going to go see what's going on."

"See what I mean?" April said once Jerry had walked away.

"Maybe," Max replied, keeping her answer short. As she slipped the vest over Houdini's head, she saw Granny move to Jerry's side. Seeing the spirit had not totally abandoned him brought her comfort. What didn't settle well was the fact that she still hadn't picked up anything on the boy they'd come to find. Every time she tried, it was as if he didn't exist. She couldn't hear the other boy because he was deaf. *Does that mean he is dead?* She shook off the thought and fastened Houdini's harness. "We're ready."

Jerry was talking to a police officer when they approached. Unfortunately, the officer didn't look pleased to see them.

Jerry nodded to them as they approached. "My name is Jerry McNeal. My fiancée April and her daughter Max are with me. We were hoping to help you with your search."

Houdini quivered as he sniffed the air.

"Max is the dog's handler. Among other things, he is a certified SARs dog."

The officer didn't look impressed. "Who told you about the search?"

"It went out over the wire. We were in the area, so the agency sent us here to help."

That got the man's attention. "What agency?"

"The one who prefers not to be named, Officer Wagner."

For a moment, Max thought Jerry knew the man, then realized he'd only been reading the name on the officer's uniform.

"And they'd bring you in on something like this?"

Granny was watching her as if seeing if she'd pick up on something that hadn't been said.

Jerry pressed on. "As I said, we were in the area, and the dog is highly trained. Do you by chance have a piece of clothing or something with Phillip's scent on it?"

Wagner frowned. "You're kidding, right?"

An image of a groundhog came to mind. Only it wasn't a statue, but a real groundhog. At that moment, Max knew the reason she hadn't picked up on the kid. *It's all a hoax. They aren't looking for a kid, they're looking for Punxsutawney Phil.* Instantly, Granny was at her side. She looped her arm through Max's arm as if reminding her to remain quiet. Max watched helplessly as Jerry stepped around the officer.

"Who's in charge here?"

"This man said the F.B.I. sent him to help us find Phil," Wagner told them.

"I never said I was with the F.B.I. I said 'agency,'" Jerry corrected.

"What's the difference?" a man in a topcoat and tails asked.

Jerry smiled. "We outrank them."

The man eyed Max. "You're saying the girl works for this agency?"

"We all do. Mr. Mayor, I don't know if you are aware of the statistics, but the first twenty-four hours are critical."

The man looked him up and down. "You know who I am?"

"The top hat kind of gave it away," Jerry told him. "Sir, if I may be bold, you sent that Amber alert out ninety minutes ago. We need to get to work organizing a search party and we need to start now."

Though their faces remained stoic, Max could feel them laughing at Jerry, who'd yet to realize they were looking for a missing rodent. Anger raced through her veins as she shrugged out of Granny's grip. *This is not okay!* she said silently before storming away with Houdini at her side. Gunter started to follow. Max stopped and held up her hand. *No, you stay with Jerry.*

Gunter looked to Granny for direction before moving to Jerry's side.

"We're looking for a groundhog," Max said, sending a mental image to Houdini.

The dog lowered his nose as he led the way through the grass and around the building and straight to the bushes on the opposite side of the street. Houdini peered at the bushes and woofed.

Max stepped around the dog and saw a bundle of brown fur curled beneath the branches.

"Max, you shouldn't go off on your own," April said, coming up behind her.

"I'm not alone," Max snapped.

April frowned. "Excuse me? What's with the attitude?"

"I'm sorry." Max shrugged. Houdini eked his way toward the bush and Max pulled him back. "Leave it."

Instantly, Houdini lowered to the ground keeping a close eye on his find.

"That's better. Listen, I know you are probably feeding off the fact that Jerry's in a bad place, but it doesn't give you a reason to yell at me. How about we both look for Phillip together?"

"We already found him."

April blinked her surprise. "What do you mean you already found him. Where is he?"

"Sleeping under the bush."

April stepped closer to the bush, peered through the branches, then stared at Max. "You're kidding, right?"

The emotions she'd been harboring spilled out in a deluge of tears. "It's true. It was all a hoax. There is no Phillip King, only Phil. Remember when Jerry told us the history of Groundhog Day and how he said Punxsutawney Phil was named after King Phillip?"

"You're saying the men were trying to trick Jerry?"

"No, I don't think they are in on it." Max sniffed. "I think it was just Granny and Bunny."

April knitted her brow. "I can see Bunny playing games, but are you sure Granny was in on it?"

"Yes, but they weren't playing games. They were teaching Jerry a lesson," Max said with a sob.

"I've never known Granny to be mean-spirited."

"She's not. At least I don't think so, but Jerry said he didn't want the spirits' help anymore. This was their way of showing him he's wrong."

April's eyes grew wide. "Is that why Jerry almost hit that little boy?"

Max nodded. "Yes, he knew something was wrong, but without their help, he couldn't tell what it was."

April narrowed her eyes. "You should have said something. Do you know what that would have done to him if he had killed that boy?"

Max brushed at the new wave of tears that trickled down her cheek. "I wanted to tell him, but Granny wouldn't let me. She promised she wouldn't let anyone get hurt."

"Anyone except Jerry," April replied.

Jerry's voice floated into her mind. *Max. Kiddo, if you can hear me, tell your mom to call Fred and tell him to fix this.*

"What is it?" April asked when Max gasped.

"I think Jerry just got arrested." Max took off running. Houdini hesitated then decided he liked this new game. Fueled by anger, Max quickly left her mother behind. As she rounded the building, she saw Jerry being helped into a police car while Granny and Bunny watched.

"That's enough!" Max yelled. It was too late. Officer Wagner closed the door, walked to the other side, got in and drove away.

Max pivoted and turned her anger on the spirits who had yet to do anything to prevent them from taking Jerry away. "Stop it, stop it right now! You're his grandmother, and grandmas aren't supposed to be mean to their kids. I know Jerry said some things, but that is no reason to take him away from us. Jerry might not be my real dad, but he's the only one who ever gave a crap. You fix this. If you don't, I don't want to be your great-granddaughter anymore." Max knew the others were watching, but she didn't care. She slid her palms together as if wiping her hands clean. "I'm serious. Bring him back or we are done."

"The girl's got spunk," Bunny said.

"Indeed," Granny agreed as both spirits disappeared.

Chapter Six

Without the aid of his cell phone, and given there were no clocks in the jail cell, Jerry had lost all track of time. That no one had read him his rights or fingerprinted him before placing him in the cell was both good and bad. Good, because that meant he'd not been officially arrested, and bad, because if they'd fingerprinted him and run him through the database, it would have immediately alerted Jefferies, meaning his boss or someone connected to him would be en route to stand on someone's desk. As it was, Jerry was currently biding his time in a jail cell with a partner who had abandoned him; at least, that was the impression, given the fact Gunter hadn't so much as looked in his direction since Officer Wagner locked the door to the cell.

What a ridiculous turn of events. He should be

helping find the missing boy, not sitting alone in a jail cell like a common criminal. Jerry tried for the umpteenth time to get a read on the child. As with each time he tried before, he got nothing.

Jerry ran a hand over his head and pulled at the back of his neck to relieve the tension. "Hey, dog, any clue what time it is?"

Gunter ignored the comment.

Jerry stood and moved to face the dog, who sat in the middle of the floor, staring at the cell door. "Yo, I know you can hear me. I see your ears twitch when I talk."

Gunter stared at him without moving.

Jerry crouched close to the dog, staring him in the eye. "I'm not sure what I did to tick you off, but this silent treatment is getting a bit ridiculous."

Gunter yawned a squeaky yawn.

Jerry raised his arms in victory. "So, you can hear me. Okay, how about you tell me what the heck is going on so I can fix it and get us out of here?"

Gunter stood and walked through the metal bars. Once on the other side, he wagged his tail as if to show him that he was free to leave anytime he wanted.

"Yeah, you might be free to go, but I'm kind of stuck in here." To prove his point, he walked into the bars. "See?"

Gunter gave him a look as if to say, *Not my problem*, then returned to the cell and lay on the floor, resting his muzzle on his front paws.

Jerry stood and walked to the bars and stared at the wall to see what had caught the dog's attention. It took a moment until he noticed a small camera flush with the opposite wall facing the cell. He sighed. *Great. Add talking to yourself to the list of charges.*

He turned away from the camera, feeling lower than he'd ever felt. He wasn't sure if it was because he was on the wrong side of the cell, the fact there was no one else in the holding cell, or what, but for some reason, even though Gunter was with him, he felt utterly alone. Even knowing there were cameras trained on him didn't help. It wasn't that he minded being alone; he'd spent most of his life alone with his own thoughts, but for as long as he could remember, he'd always felt one or more spirits hovering nearby even when he couldn't see them. Today, he felt nothing. Suddenly and irrationally, he felt like a child who was afraid of the dark. Jerry ran his hand over his head in an attempt to settle his nerves.

"Granny? Are you here?" He knew she wasn't near as he couldn't feel her presence, nor had he felt her near since leaving DuBois, but he thought maybe if he said her name, she'd appear. The overwhelming sense of loneliness was unsettling. A desperation set in, leaving him grasping for some sort of normalcy. "Bunny?"

Nothing.

"Hello? Is anyone here?" When no spirits showed themselves, Jerry walked to the door and stared directly at the camera. "Hello? I have rights. I want to make a phone call!"

Nothing.

Jerry palmed his hand against the bar and walked to the other side of the room. He kicked the bench, then thought about sending his fist into the wall. He recalled the look on April's face as Wagner led him away, and shoved his hands into his pockets.

A fine mess you've got yourself into this time, McNeal. Not true; this wasn't his fault. He racked his brain and couldn't recall doing anything wrong.

Jerry thought about the little boy and how close he'd come to killing him, then shook off the chill that raced up and down his arms. If not for Max and April...

He was close to panic and wished for his cell phone so he could call for help. Only the help he was thinking of wouldn't set him free of anything but the inner turmoil that swirled inside his mind.

Doc. A voice inside his head laughed at the absurdity. *Even the good doctor has abandoned you. That's not true. Doc abandoned himself, not me.*

Not wishing to be alone with his thoughts, Jerry returned to the wall of bars and looked directly into the camera once more. "Yo, I know my rights! Either arrest me or let me go!"

A moment passed before the outer door to the hallway clicked open.

Officer Wagner entered carrying a clipboard. "Sheriff wants to know if you'll submit to a tox screen."

Jerry blinked his disbelief. "You think I'm drunk?"

"I don't know what you are. What I do know is you were not making sense when we picked you up, and we've watched you talk to yourself repeatedly since you've been in."

Jerry glanced at Gunter, halfway wishing the dog would show himself so Wagner would know he wasn't a nut job. He also knew a negative tox screen would not necessarily get him released. If they thought him to be a danger to others, it would give them cause to keep him locked up until they could arrange a psych consult. It being a Friday, that could mean he'd be locked up for days. The thought of being alone with his thoughts for that long caused his heart to race. Jerry forced a smile. "I'd like to make a phone call."

Wagner wiggled the clipboard. "You're refusing the blood test?"

"Only if you're refusing to allow me a phone call," Jerry countered.

"I'll check with the sheriff." Wagner turned on his heels and left without another word.

Jerry turned and winked at Gunter, who'd been

exceptionally well-behaved during Wagner's visit. "One call to Fred, and I'll be set free."

Gunter yawned.

As if the yawn had conveyed a silent message, it suddenly struck him that while he'd spoken with his boss hundreds of times, he'd always reached the man by using speed dial. Jerry racked his brain, trying to glean the man's number. Nothing came to mind. *Okay, no big deal, I'll just call April and have her convey the message.* It occurred to him she'd already had plenty of time to do just that since he'd been in.

Jerry recalled the look on April's face as Wagner helped him into the car. A mingled look of shock and anger. *I reminded her of her ex-husband. That's the reason she hasn't called Fred; she's disappointed in me.* The realization made him more determined to make the call. Fred could wait; he needed April to hear his voice and to convince her he was nothing like Randy.

The sound of footsteps had Jerry hurrying to the other side of the room.

Wagner shook his head. "No can do."

Jerry was incensed. "You're refusing to let me make a phone call?"

"You can make all the calls you want. Nothing's getting out. Cell service is down all over the city. Land lines and internet too. See for yourself," Wagner said, handing Jerry his cell phone.

Jerry took the phone and swiped to call April, only to reach a recording telling him the call had failed. Jerry frowned. "How is it possible for everything to go out at once?"

"No clue. But unless you have some divine intervention, you aren't making a call until service comes up."

"Wait," Jerry said as Wagner turned to leave. "How'd you get my cell phone?"

"Miss Buchannan brought it."

"April was here?"

Wagner smiled. "Feisty woman you got there. She almost ended up in there with you."

"Didn't she show you my badge?"

"She did. Then she threatened to shove it where the sun doesn't shine when we told her we needed to verify it was real."

Jerry stifled a chuckle. "Where is she now?"

"She and the girl are probably getting their pictures taken with the mayor."

"You mean they found the kid?"

"Kid?" Wagner shook his head. "You know, buddy, you'd think you would have learned your lesson by now. They aren't going to let you out if you keep acting delusional."

"What in the…" Jerry checked his tone. "We came here to help find a missing kid. Just tell me if Phillip King has been found."

"There's no missing kid, and we didn't send out

an Amber alert."

No missing kid? "Wait, you said your people were looking for him."

Wagner moved to block the camera and lowered his voice. "We were looking for Phil."

Jerry bobbed his head. "That's right, Phillip King."

"No, not Phillip King. Punxsutawney Phil. The groundhog was out for a meet and greet today. Someone set off a firecracker and scared the little guy so bad, he took off. It has happened a time or two." Wagner shrugged. "We like to keep these things under wraps in case we need to find a replacement groundhog. People like Phil. They like the magic of believing we've found some magic elixir that makes him live a hundred lives. Anyway, it was Miss Buchanan's daughter who found him. Her, and that dog of hers. I think the mayor's going to give them the key to the city."

"They'd probably settle for a get-out-of-jail-free card," Jerry quipped.

"I'll pass that along to the sheriff." Wagner reached for the cell phone.

Jerry pulled it back. "No reason I can't keep it since it doesn't work, right?"

Wagner studied him for a moment before walking away without comment.

Jerry moved to the bench, holding the phone like a hard-won prize. He swiped to bring the phone to life. Looking in his contacts, he tried to call April. The call failed. He tried Max, Fred, Seltzer, and even attempted to call Barney, all to no avail. Opening up Messenger, he attempted to send several messages and received a failed message error with each attempt.

Jerry sighed. Wagner was right; the only way he would get a call through was through divine intervention. That thought stayed with him as he pocketed the phone and lay stretched out on the bench. While Granny had promised she'd always be near, he couldn't feel her. Even before he could actually see her individual spirit, others always hovered near. But not today. This was a jail cell – places like this were normally full of activity, and yet he felt nothing. Yes, something was most definitely off.

Jerry intertwined his fingers, laid his hands across his chest, and closed his eyes. As he lay there, he retraced the events of the day, stopping when both April and Max called his name. *They called to me before either the dog or the boy came into view. Not just Max, but April as well, both at the same time.* He hadn't missed anything; he'd been in the zone, watching the road and surroundings during the entire drive. Max and April couldn't have known what was going to happen unless someone told them. He replayed that moment over and over in his mind until he was sure.

My gift is gone!

Jerry sat bolt upright as the realization hit him. Panic gripped him as his palms began to sweat. So many times, he'd wished to be done with the gift. Wished the powers that be had chosen someone else. And now, as he sat behind bars, knowing he was but a mere mortal, the emptiness he felt engulfed him until, at last, he thought he would implode. He gripped the bench, digging his fingertips into the wood, hoping the pain would prove this wasn't all just a horrible nightmare. He needed to feel something when all around him there was nothing.

Tears filled his eyes, blurring his vision. As the blackness threatened to overtake him, he opened his mouth and uttered a single word.

"Help."

Gunter's howls broke through the darkness, beckoning like a lighthouse, giving him a safe harbor.

Jerry turned toward the sound as Gunter sidled up to him, wiggling and slathering him with ghostly drool as if saying, *All you had to do was ask.*

"It took you long enough." Granny's voice was clear, and he could feel her presence all around him.

"It sure did," Bunny said, appearing next to Granny. "I thought we'd lost you forever."

One by one, spirits he'd encountered over the years materialized in the cell, each filling his senses and letting him know he was no longer alone.

Chapter Seven

The spiritual hug was short-lived. Jerry soon found himself alone in the cell except for Gunter and the spirit of his grandmother. Jerry looked at the camera and realized anyone watching would know he'd reached his breaking point. "I guess they'll have enough video proof to lock me up for a time."

"That camera only sees what we want it to see," Granny told him.

"So what, has this been some kind of test?"

"No."

"Then what was it? I've never felt so alone in my life."

"You weren't alone. You still had April and Max, plus Gunter was here."

"I couldn't feel them. Any of them, not even Gunter, and he was with me all the time."

"Gunter was here because Max told him to stay with you."

"Max? What does she have to do with this?"

"Max had nothing to do with this." Granny waved her hands. "But she is a gifted child. It didn't take her long to figure out what was going on. I'm afraid she's not too happy with us."

"Max is mad at me? I guess that would explain why she blocked me."

Granny patted his knee. "She's not mad at you, Jerry. She's mad at me and the spirit world. She blocked you because I told her to."

This was all so confusing. "You told Max to block me?"

"Not in so many words, but I told her she couldn't help you."

"I'm afraid I'm not following you."

"You lost your faith, Jerry."

"My faith?"

"In the spirit world. You've wavered before, but this was the first time you outright denounced it."

"I'm afraid you're mistaken," Jerry said, running a hand over his head.

Bunny appeared before them. Sitting at a desk wearing a no-nonsense pantsuit and spectacles, she had a stenograph machine in front of her. She hit a button and printed off a sheet of paper. "Here it is right here, and I quote, 'Listen, I don't care how many downloads you get, you are not to write articles about my family.' Then I said you can't do that and you said 'I forbid it. I don't want any help from you or anyone else. Take my family out of the Spirit Pipeline.' Bunny tossed the paper into the air and it disappeared. "Of course, we didn't actually remove Max or April because of the whole free will and how you're not allowed to make decisions for them and all, but we granted you your wish."

Jerry recalled the conversation. He glanced at Gunter, who was sitting and intently watching the proceedings. "I said I didn't want any help. Is that why I couldn't feel Gunter with me?"

Granny nodded.

"I almost hit that little boy."

Another nod. "You would have killed him and the dog if not for Max and April."

That was a piece of the puzzle he had yet to figure out. "I understand Max knowing something would happen, but April called my name at the same time."

"They both heard me tell them to call your name."

"Why not just tell them to tell me to stop?"

"Because that would have been helping you." This time, it was Bunny who spoke. "If they'd told you to stop, it would be divine intervention, but since they called your name, you still had a choice."

"You knew something was wrong, Jerry. You just didn't have your normal guidance."

Jerry was incensed. "You used an innocent child to teach me a lesson?"

"It was my idea," Bunny said, bobbing her head. "The stakes were high, so we needed to make sure you knew the severity of your decision."

Jerry stood and paced the cell. "You almost got that boy killed. You need to stay out of…"

Bunny cut him off. "Careful, Jer. You see how that's worked out for you thus far."

Jerry sucked in a breath. "The Spirit Pipeline has been nothing but trouble since you started it."

"You got me all wrong, Jer. The Spirit Pipeline is as old as the hills. I didn't start it. I just took it over." Bunny seemed to consider her words. "I may have spruced it up a bit…think of it as a new and improved addition."

"It's nothing but trouble," Jerry countered.

Bunny pulled herself taller. "On the contrary, it gets people out of trouble."

"How do you figure?"

"Think of it as kind of a hearing aid for the dearly departed. Anything plugged into the pipeline gets streamlined into a high-tech prayer list. When you ask for help, your request creates a frequency, which is then inputted into the pipeline and sent out to spirits who are available to help."

"It's true," Granny agreed.

"And what, we can just turn it off on a whim?"

Bunny started to answer, when Granny held up a

hand to stop her. "No, if that was the case, the spirits would have abandoned you years ago. This is not the first time you've renounced your gift."

"It's true." Bunny snapped her fingers, producing a stack of papers. "I believe the total count is five thousand, seven hundred and twenty-three times. Would you like me to read them back to you?"

Jerry waved her off. "No, I'll take your word for it."

"But this was the first time you directly forbade us to help, so we had to listen. You needed to see what your life would be like without our help. You needed to experience what that hollow void would feel like."

"That's exactly what it felt like," Jerry replied.

"What's that, Jer?" Bunny asked.

"I felt as if I was all alone. Even though Gunter was here all along, I couldn't feel his presence. My life was a big nothing. I couldn't feel April, Max, or anyone in the building. All around me was just like a huge wall of nothing blocking my every thought."

"And now?" Granny asked.

"I feel normal again."

Bunny shook her head. "Nothing about you is normal."

Granny nodded her agreement. "So you're saying you want our help?"

"I do," Jerry replied without hesitation.

Bunny grinned. "Even mine?"

Jerry sighed. "All of it. I want things to be like they were before, whatever that entails."

"Oh, goodie." Bunny clapped her hands together like a child who'd just won a prize, then stopped mid-clap. "Oh, my, I'd better get to it."

"Get to what?" Jerry asked.

"Retracting your DNR," Bunny said and disappeared.

Jerry gulped. "You're telling me I have a Do Not Resuscitate order?"

"Had," Granny said. "I'm sure Bunny has sent out the edited edition by now. Things like that are big news. She's sure to get a lot of downloads."

"I thought DNRs are just for medical personnel to go by."

"They are." Granny winked. "Who do you think guides their hands?"

Jerry's cell rang, announcing Fred's call.

Granny smiled and gave him a peck on the cheek. "Bunny works fast. Things are back online already. Take the call, Jerry. Mr. Jefferies has been mighty worried about you."

Feeling more like himself, Jerry chuckled. "Fred doesn't worry. He has people who worry for him."

"That's not true, Jerry. Your denouncement didn't just affect you. It affected everyone you'd ever interacted with. Fred felt the loss just as greatly as others whose lives you touch." Granny motioned toward the phone. "Take the call. You'll see."

Jerry swiped to answer. "Hello."

"McNeal!" Fred's voice was full of concern. "April called hours ago to tell me you'd been arrested. I've been trying to reach you, but it seems as if the area was under some sort of cyber-attack. Barney and I have been beside ourselves with worry since every mode of communication has been blocked. Hold tight. We'll get you out. Before I go, I want to make sure you're okay."

Jerry smiled. "I am now."

Once communication was restored, it didn't take long for things to return to normal. Jerry heard footsteps in the hallway and knew Wagner was on the way even before the man came into view.

"Mr. McNeal, you are free to go." Wagner unlocked the cell door and held it open for him. "It seems as if we were mistaken, and somehow, an Amber alert was sent out to select devices. The mayor asked me to convey his apologies and to let you know he would be having a word with our tech person to see how something like this happened."

"I spoke to my boss, and he seems to think it was some kind of cyber-attack," Jerry said, giving the department an out.

"That would make as much sense as anything," Wagner said, letting the door slam. The man stopped halfway down the hall. "As for the other thing, I hope you don't take offense."

Jerry lifted a brow. "The other thing, as in thinking I had a screw loose?"

Wagner shifted his feet. "Put yourself in my shoes. Would you have thought any different?"

"I've been in your shoes," Jerry told him. "Not to mention I told you I had ID."

"You didn't have it on you, and the badge…you're telling me you would have believed me if I showed it to you and told you I was the Lead Paranormal Investigator for the DOD?"

"Since I am who I am, I would have known you were telling the truth." Jerry sighed. "But if I were you, I probably would have thought it to be a fake badge and wanted to verify I was who I said I was."

Wagner smiled. "You can't tell me this is the first time you've been questioned."

Jerry shook his head. "Questioned no, detained yes."

Wagner began walking once more. "Perhaps the DOD needs to send out a memo to all departments to let them know."

"Doubtful. They like to keep things like this under wraps."

Wagner laughed. "Let me guess, now you're going to zap us all with your pen so we forget you were even here?"

"No, I leave the lockdown to my boss."

"That'd be Mr. Jefferies?"

"You spoke with him?"

"Nope, that'd be my boss, and he didn't look happy when he hung up the phone."

"Jefferies has that effect on people."

"Sounds like a pain to work for," Wagner noted.

"My boss doesn't like it when people interfere with company business. He sent me to do a job, and I got locked in jail; you might see where that would rattle his cage."

"He said if you need anything, we are to comply. Must be nice having that kind of clout."

Jerry glanced at Granny, who'd followed them from the cell. "Sometimes, everyone needs a little help."

Chapter Eight

April and Max were waiting in the Durango when he exited the building. The second he stepped outside, the driver's door opened. April ran to greet him.

Jerry welcomed her embrace, enjoying the solidity of her hug.

"Oh, Jerry, I'm so sorry. I tried to get them to let you out, but they threatened to lock me up. I would have pushed harder, but I was worried about Max."

"You did the right thing, Ladybug." Jerry released her and wrapped his arm around her as they walked to the SUV. "How's Max holding up?"

"She's been quiet. She feels responsible for you getting arrested."

"That was not on her," Jerry said firmly.

"I know," April sniffed.

Jerry stopped when he realized she was crying. "Are you okay?"

"I am now. I told Max the same thing. Maybe she'll believe you."

As they neared the Durango, Max got out, leaving the door open for Houdini to join her.

The young dog jumped out, spinning in eager circles as he barked his greeting and lapped at the sides of Gunter's muzzle.

"Hi, Gunter," April said when Gunter joined in the chorus. "Good job watching over Jerry."

Jerry looked directly at Max. "Thanks for sending him."

"Granny told me not to help, but I didn't want you to be alone," Max said, glancing over her shoulder.

Jerry followed her gaze and saw both Granny and Bunny waiting in the back of the SUV.
He smiled at them then returned his attention to Max. "You did good."

Max's eyes grew wide. "You're not mad at them for what they did?"

April frowned. "Mad at who? What am I missing?"

"Granny and Bunny are in the Durango," Jerry replied.

"Oh," April replied. "Max said they are the reason you were in jail. If she's right, maybe you should be mad at them."

"They may have played a part, but the brunt of this falls on me. I said some things I shouldn't have said. Granny and Bunny were showing me what life would be like without them." Jerry went on to give a brief explanation of what he'd said and what had taken place inside the cell, stopping short of describing his breaking point. He looked at both April and Max, including them in the next part. "Bottom line, we need the spirits to guide us. I was foolish to think otherwise."

"Are you good, Jerry?"

Jerry thought of Doc. "Golden."

April smiled. "You should call him."

Jerry furrowed his brow. "Call who?"

"Doc. I know that reminded you of him."

"It did." He didn't know if she was hinting that maybe he needed to talk to his friend or not, but it was the second time he'd thought of the man today. "I'll give him a call when we get settled. Speaking of getting on the road, we need a plan. I'm not going to meet with Sinclair until the end of the week. We have time to take a quick tour of the town and see Gobbler's Knob before we leave."

Max glanced at April. "We've already seen all the statues. The mayor took us."

"Max didn't want to go, but I made her." April shrugged her apologies. "The mayor was grateful to Max and Houdini for helping find the groundhog. I thought it would make a good photo op and be good for their portfolio."

"You also thought if you got in good with the mayor, he might be able to pull some strings to get me out," Jerry replied.

April shrugged. "I figured it couldn't hurt."

Jerry smiled. "That's my girl, always thinking."

"Uncle Fred would have gotten you out," Max said sourly. "It was only a matter of time."

"The spirits knew that. That's why they disabled all communication," Jerry told her. "Did you have fun?"

Max offered a reluctant nod.

"Good. I'm glad you went. Both of you. This was not the mayor's fault. The people of the town, law enforcement included, are a great bunch. You walk through town during the annual groundhog event, and they'll show you. One thing that stood out from my time here was how festive the mood was. It reminded me of Christmas, only, instead of saying Merry Christmas, locals and visitors alike would pass people on the sidewalk and wish them a Happy Groundhog Day. The next morning, after a long night of partying on top of the hill, people weren't sulking because an overgrown rat promised Mother Nature would blast them with six more weeks of winter. No, they walked through town visiting shops and drinking hot chocolate and cold beer. The park is packed with vendor booths and chainsaw art, and the air is filled with a combination of woodsmoke and sawdust."

April smiled. "I believe you told us all this before."

"I did? Did I mention the fact that the mayor mingles with the crowd? Wearing a top hat and tails, he's escorted through town like royalty as he stops and converses with his subjects. The police aren't out arresting people for being drunk in public, though half of the people probably are. No, they are just making sure things don't get out of hand and ushering them to the coffee tent if they feel they've imbibed a bit too much."

"It sounds like we might need to come back in February," April mused.

"We didn't get to see Gobbler's Knob yet," Max said. "The phones came up before we had a chance."

"Then Gobbler's Knob it is." Jerry waved a hand toward the Durango and watched as Max and the dogs piled inside. He shut the door and walked to the other side. He started to open the door for April then hesitated and pulled her into his arms instead.

"Are you sure you're okay?" she whispered.

"Just making sure you're real," he replied.

"You put up a good front for Max, but I can tell whatever happened inside got to you."

"They just reminded me how much I hate being alone."

"PTSD?"

"PTSD on steroids."

"You're not, you know."

"Not what?"

"Not alone. And you better get used to it, because between me and Max and the dogs, you'll never be alone again." April looked up at him and smiled. "I'm serious, Jerry. I know how this works. If I die before you, I'm coming back just to haunt you."

Jerry laughed. "I'm not sure whether to be flattered or terrified."

April winked. "Either way, you don't ever have to worry about being alone."

He kissed her, then opened the door. As he waited for her to get in, he looked to see Granny and Bunny grinning at him. His gaze swept over Max and the dogs and then rested on April. He leaned in, kissing her once more. Pulling away, he sighed a contented sigh. "I'm okay with that."

Jerry walked around the Durango, climbed into the driver's seat and buckled his seatbelt. As he pushed the button to start the vehicle, he reached for April's hand. "For the record, I don't want you going anywhere."

April pulled her hand free and placed it alongside his cheek. "Right back atcha, McNeal."

Max leaned forward. "What about me?"

"You're not going anywhere!" Jerry and April said at once.

Gunter and Houdini woofed their agreement.

It didn't take long to get to the turnoff to

Gobbler's Knob. As he drove past the Chevrolet dealership, Jerry pointed to the small green sign that read "Gobbler's Knob, 1.3 miles." "There's the sign."

"You're right." April held her phone out the window to take a photo of the sign as he turned right on Woodland Ave Ext. "It's really nothing like the movie."

"It's not. But that's not the city's fault. They relied on the groundhog to predict the weather long before Bill Murray made the movie." Jerry kept the speed at twenty-five miles per hour, noting the houses that lined the two-lane street.

"I'm sure the movie helped," April said.

"I'm sure it did," Jerry agreed. Several moments passed until they rounded the bend and the road opened to farmland. A few moments later, the speed limit increased to forty. Finally, he saw the stone pillars that marked the park-like entrance for Gobbler's Knob. He turned into the empty gravel lot, parking close to the wooden split rail fence that faced the stage and bandstand area where Punxsutawney Phil made his predictions. A banner in the center showed a photo of the groundhog, along with the words "Home of Punxy Phil," further claiming Punxsutawney, PA to be the *Weather Capital of the World*. Jerry took in the empty stage and noted the yard, which was pressed full of eager tourists the last time he'd been here. He turned off the Durango as they all piled out. "It is a lot more festive during the ceremony."

"Are you kidding?" April exclaimed, taking it all in. "This is so cool. Carrie's going to want pictures! Max, we'll start with a picture of you and Houdini on the stage."

Houdini barked and wagged his tail, excited to be included.

Gunter, on the other hand, yawned and looked at them as if to say, *You kids, go on and have your fun; I'm staying here with the adults.*

Bunny appeared next to them, clapping her hands with girlish delight. She tugged on Granny's arm, pulling her toward the stage. "Come on, Betty Lou, I can't wait to tell everyone I was on the same stage as Bill Murray."

Gunter growled a grumbling growl.

April laughed. "I can't see any of them, but I can clearly picture what just happened."

"You mean that Gunter thinks we should tell her this isn't the same stage?"

April bobbed her head. "She sounded so happy. I don't think we should tell her."

"I agree. Listen, you two go get your pictures. I need to call Seltzer to let him know we aren't coming and my folks to let them know we are."

"Let your mom know we don't mind staying at a hotel," April said.

"I'll pass it along." Normally, his mother

wouldn't hear of such a thing, but then again, since they hadn't told him of the move, they could be living in an apartment for all he knew. Even before April, Max and the dogs started down the path to the bandstand area, Granny and Bunny appeared on the stage. Jerry leaned against the side of the Durango and stared at his phone, wondering who to call first. Searching his contacts, he pressed to call his mother.

Lori answered on the third ring. "Are you okay?"

"Yes, Mom, I'm okay."

"Good. Talk to your father. I don't want to get the phone wet. Wayne, come get my phone. No, it's Jerry. No, hold it close. I put it on speaker so I can hear."

"Oh, for Pete's sake. Why don't you just talk to him?"

"Did I call at a bad time? If I did, I can call back."

"No, you're good. Your mother's in the pool and is worried about getting her phone wet."

"If you two are at the center, I can call back," Jerry insisted. "That, or you can call me back when you get home."

"We are home!" Lori's voice sang out. "Tell him."

"We moved," his father said without explanation.

Jerry decided not to let on that he already knew. "You left The Villages?"

"No, we just decided it was time for an upgrade."

"Mike and Barb's neighbor was selling her place

and offered us an incredible deal," Lori added.

"Mike and Barb are the ones we play cards with," Wayne clarified. "Their neighbor's husband, Harold, passed, and Carol moved back to Ohio. The kids are building her an in-law suite, and she gets to be near her grandkids. They were such a nice couple. Harold had a great handicap. Hated to see him go, but happy to have gotten this deal."

"Is this handicap what killed him?"

"What?"

"Your dad's talking golf, Jerry. Harold was as fit as a fiddle until he had a heart attack on the seventh hole."

"Widow maker," Wayne said.

"Yep, a heart attack will do that," Jerry agreed.

"No. I meant what killed him was what's called a widow maker. It's an artery in the heart. Ugly little ba…"

"Wayne, watch your language. Max might be listening."

"Max isn't listening," Jerry assured them. "Speaking of Max."

"What's wrong with Max?" Lori blurted.

"Nothing's wrong with Max other than she'd like to spend a little time with her grandparents." While he hadn't planned on telling them over the phone, it seemed the perfect segue into telling of their planned visit.

"Grandparents?" Lori's voice was shrill. "Does

that mean you've finally asked April to marry you?"

"I did."

"Bout time you decided to make an honest woman out of her," Wayne agreed.

"When's the wedding?!" Lori yelled.

"Great Scott, woman, if you want to talk to him, climb out of that pool and take the phone. Haven't lived here but a moment, and the neighbors are already thinking we're heathens."

Jerry chuckled. "We haven't set a date yet. April doesn't want a big wedding. Listen, I need to come to Florida for business. April, Max and I are in Pennsylvania, so they will be coming with me. We can catch up when we get there in a couple of days."

Lori squealed.

"That got her out of the pool." Wayne snorted. "Old gal nearly fell off her raft."

"Tell Mom we don't need to stay there. I can get a hotel or rent something."

"You know your mother better than that. The main reason we even considered moving was because it gives us the extra room. Max's room is the first one she had me paint. Looks like a Barbie threw up in there."

Jerry glanced across the way to where Max was posing with Houdini while April snapped her photo. Never in the time he'd known her had he seen her play with dolls. "Mom does realize Max is thirteen, doesn't she?"

"You've seen your mother's golf cart. All your mother heard was Max is a girl."

Jerry recalled the pink monstrosity that looked like it was plucked straight from a Barbie catalog. "Do me a favor. Tell Mom not to buy Max any clothes."

"Let me guess, Max is one of those tomboy types."

"She's thirteen. Thirteen-year-old girls like to pick out their clothes."

"I'll let her know. Listen, you know how your mom frets. I'd better go and help her before she worries herself sick."

"Sorry to spring the trip on you like this," Jerry said sincerely.

"We'll get by just fine. Don't ever apologize for coming to see us."

"Hey, before I go, I probably should get your new address."

"We're in the Village of Hillsborough on Vineland Street. I'll text you the address along with directions."

"Okay, Pop, I'll see you soon," Jerry said, ending the call. Heaving a sigh, he dialed Seltzer's number to give him the bad news.

***

"How'd it go?" April asked when he reached her.

"Seltzer took it okay. He understands the job. Depending on how long we're in Florida, we could still see them."

April cocked an eyebrow. "Oh?"

"They booked a cruise and will be flying to Florida next week."

"Oh, how fun."

"You like cruises?"

"Don't know. I've never been on one. I think I'd like it, but the only boat I've ever been on was the riverboat in Frankenmuth. I liked it okay, but then again, I didn't have to worry about rogue waves."

A surge of excitement coursed through him. "We could see if there are any cabins left and go with them."

April's eyes sparkled. "Do you think there are any left?"

"I'll look into it."

Houdini woofed.

Gunter snarled as Max jumped off the wooden stage and followed Houdini into the woods.

"Max!" April's words fell on deaf ears.

Jerry started to advise April to wait and knew he'd be wasting his breath. He forged ahead with April following close behind.

Max stood at the edge of the brush with Granny and Gunter as Houdini dug at something under the brush.

April grabbed hold of Jerry's arm. "Tell me he hasn't found more bones."

Jerry inched forward, trying to see what had

captured the dog's attention. Picking up a good-sized branch, he pulled the foliage away. Tossing the branch to the side, he glanced at Max. "Call him off."

"Houdini, leave it," Max said firmly.

The young dog backed out of the brush, and Max took hold of his harness.

Jerry looked at Max. "Got him?"

Max nodded.

Jerry rustled the brush. A second later, a plump groundhog scurried from under the brush and hurried off in the opposite direction. Houdini whined but made no move to give chase.

Max beamed.

"I hope you're still smiling when we get to Florida," Jerry said.

"Why wouldn't she be?" April asked. "Is it your parents? Do they not want us to come?"

"Stop your fretting, Ladybug. They are thrilled we're coming. They moved so they would have enough room for their new granddaughter to come visit." Jerry smiled at Max. "Mom even had Dad paint your room."

Max's smile waned as she read him. "Ugh, is it really that pink?"

Jerry laughed. "Kiddo, whatever you're picturing in that pretty little head of yours, I suggest you double it."

Chapter Nine

Jerry reached across the console and placed his hand on April's arm.

She opened her eyes and raised the seat she'd been sleeping in. "Is it time for me to drive?"

"No. We are almost there."

"You were supposed to wake me."

"I wasn't tired. Besides, you were sleeping so soundly that your snores helped keep me awake."

"Very funny. How much longer?"

"About ten miles. I thought you might like to get your wits about you before we get there."

April yawned and stretched her arms. "What I'd like is a shower."

"Knowing my mother, she already has a bath ready for you. What was that look for?" Jerry asked when April frowned.

"Nothing."

"Not nothing, and I'm too tired to guess. Tell me."

April stared out the window as she spoke. "You said your parents bought the place so it would have enough room when we come visit. They painted a room specifically for Max, and now you expect your mother has already run me a bath."

"Yes?"

"Your parents sound great, and yet the way you talk, you barely saw them when you were a kid. How can they be nurturing and uncaring at the same time? I don't care how much my kid liked my parents, I wouldn't allow her to live with them if I was alive and well."

"I got to see my parents anytime I wanted. My mother and I have always been okay, but my pop and I got along better when our time was limited. I was a difficult kid."

"You were a kid. All kids are difficult."

Jerry slowed for a red light. "Not all kids talk to spirits and have insight into the future."

"Max does, and I didn't throw her away."

"My parents didn't throw me away. I'm not saying they did the right thing, but it was better than living in a house where everyone was constantly walking on eggshells. At least when I was at Granny's, she encouraged me to be who I was. So, I just started staying with her, and no one seemed to mind." Jerry glanced in the mirror. Though his grandmother was listening, she made no move to join in the conversation. The light turned green. Jerry pressed on the gas. "What's this really about?"

"I guess I'm just scared they won't like us."

Now, they were getting somewhere. He lowered his voice to a whisper. "You're worried about them not liking Max because she's like me."

April nodded.

"It took some time, but my parents have learned to accept me for who I am. I've told them all about Max. They can't wait to meet you both. When they do, I promise they will adore you both just as much as I do."

"And if they don't?" April's voice was barely above a whisper.

"Then we will leave. I'm serious about that. If at any point you don't feel welcome, just say the word, and we'll pack up and go. Okay?"

April nodded. "Okay, Jerry."

"Good. How about waking Max so she can officially meet her grandparents."

April giggled. "They aren't officially her grandparents yet."

Jerry smiled as he turned onto his parents' street. "You try telling them that."

As if having a sixth sense about their son's impending arrival, both Wayne and Lori were sitting on the front porch when they pulled into the driveway. Jerry glanced at April as he shifted into park. "Ready to do this?"

April stifled a yawn. "No, but I guess I don't have a choice."

"You've got this." Jerry unfastened his seatbelt and opened the door. As he got out, he took in the well-manicured corner lot and beautiful cream stucco home that looked to be triple the size of the small, manageable house they'd previously retired to.

Wayne and Lori hurried to greet them, oblivious to Gunter, who was currently releasing an invisible stream on the closest palm tree.

"Keep Houdini away from the palm trees," Granny said as she passed. "They don't take too kindly to dog urine." She tucked her hand through the crook of Bunny's arm. "Come on, Bunny, let's go see the house."

Jerry turned to greet his parents. "Nice digs."

Wayne beamed under the compliment. "Your mother calls it her dream home."

"That's a lot of yard to take care of in the Florida heat," Jerry said as his gaze trailed over the corner lot.

"I manage just fine," Wayne replied. "Besides, the back is mostly concrete and pool."

Lori moved in for a hug. "Don't let your father fool you." She pecked him on the cheek and wiped the lipstick off with her thumb.

"Fool me about what?"

"We have a lawn crew who takes care of it for us. Wayne hasn't cut a single blade of grass since we moved in."

Wayne shrugged. "We decided since you aren't hurting for money, we might as well spend a little of your inheritance. Lori has someone come in and clean once a week while she gets her nails done, and I get to sip a beer while I watch someone else mow my grass."

His mother snickered. "He's usually drinking that beer while sitting in his golf cart. That was one of the many things that sold us on this house. Wayne's favorite golf course is just a short cart ride away."

"Good for you," Jerry said sincerely. "I'm glad you are both living your best life."

"The only thing that makes him happier than being near the golf course is that the house has a golf cart garage." Lori pointed to the small door that sat just to the left of the larger door. "You should see him strutting when he exits that door."

The passenger door shut. Jerry felt his own sense of pride as April rounded the front of the Durango.

Lori smiled. "April, it is so good to finally meet you."

April stopped just out of the woman's reach. "It's good to meet you too."

The side door opened. Max got out.

Lori's eyes lit up. "And there's little Max."

Jerry held his breath.

Instead of balking at the comment, Max moved straight to Lori, wrapping her arms around the woman. "Granny has told me so much about you, and you too," she said, looking at Jerry's father.

And there it was, out in the open for everyone to hear. While he'd told them Max had the gift, he'd not gone into the details about what the girl could do. Jerry held back, watching his parents to see how they would react to the news.

Lori didn't flinch. "You mean to tell me you can speak to the dead?"

"Yep. I can see them too, just like Jerry," Max said proudly. "Mom can hear them, but she can't see them. Not yet anyway. Granny said it's only a matter of time."

"Well, it certainly does sound as if you've been chatting with my mother. She used to go on and on about Jerry's gifts." Lori looked over at Wayne as they all stood waiting to see how the man would respond.

His father looked directly at him, and for a moment, Jerry was a kid again. A memory flashed of his time sitting in the cell and the reason for it. Max was right to approach things straightforwardly. He shook off the memory and pulled himself taller.

Wayne grinned. "I guess we know why you fell for them."

Jerry relaxed. "It's one of the reasons."

Gunter woofed as a small lizard scurried across the driveway.

Houdini whined.

Max backed out of Lori's embrace and clapped the side of her leg. "Houdini, come."

Houdini jumped down and raced to Max's side.

Lori gasped. "That's that little pup who tinkled on my rug?"

Jerry nodded. "He's fully housebroken and nearly as big as Gunter now."

"Is he here?" Wayne asked.

Gunter moved up beside Wayne and leaned into the man's leg.

Wayne's face paled as he looked to where the ghostly K-9 stood. "He is here, isn't he?"

Jerry nodded.

Wayne reached out to Gunter, sighed, and pulled back his hand. "I can feel him, but I can't feel him. Does that make sense?"

"It does," Jerry replied.

Lori frowned. "Not to me."

Gunter moved to Lori's side, brushing against her. She swallowed and nodded her understanding. "That puff of wind is the dog?"

Jerry grinned. "It is."

Lori made her own unsuccessful attempt at petting Gunter. "Well, don't that beat all."

April yawned.

Lori's manners kicked in. "You poor thing, you must be exhausted. Jerry can unload your suitcases. Come on, I'll show you girls your rooms."

"Oh, she's a beauty," Wayne said as Jerry's gaze followed after April. "Bet she squeals when you get on her."

Why, of all the ... The heat rose in Jerry's cheeks. He turned to give his father a piece of his mind and saw him checking out the Durango.

Gunter smiled a K-9 grin and looked at Jerry as if to say, *Boy, he had you going for a moment there*.

Jerry ignored the imagined quip as he opened the door for his dad to see inside.

Wayne slid into the driver's seat. "A step up from that roller skate you used to drive."

"Roller skate?"

"That thing you were driving the last time you were here."

Jerry recalled the car he'd despised at first and finally made peace with shortly before returning it. "It was a rental."

"Good. Because that was a little sissy car. This is a man's car."

"Put your foot on the brake." Jerry reached through and started the Durango.

The moment the Hemi rumbled to life, Gunter appeared in the seat next to his father.

"That's what I'm talking about." Wayne continued to look about, testing knobs and nodding his approval, then turned his attention to the roof of the vehicle. "What, no sunroof?"

"The agency thought I could do with something better than a sunroof."

"I don't know how a storage compartment could be better than seeing the stars," Wayne grumbled.

"Watch your head," Jerry said as he pushed the button to open the overhead compartment. Though he couldn't see his father's expression, the excited energy and string of appreciative expletives spoke volumes. "Yep, that's pretty much what I said when I first saw it."

His father's fingers trailed over the small arsenal. "Are you expecting a war?"

"The agency likes me to be prepared for any emergency."

"I'd say that would do it," Wayne agreed. "In my day, driving a company car meant driving a Buick."

"I guess the agency has a slightly larger budget."

"And they just give you this beast to drive because you can see ghosts."

Jerry wanted to argue the fact and tell his father there was more to it than that, but the truth was that those words summed it up pretty well. "Pretty much."

"Well, if that don't beat all." Wayne pushed the button to turn off the engine, then lowered his hand and sat staring out the windshield. "Son, I know I didn't always know how to handle this gift of yours…"

"It's okay, Dad," Jerry said, offering his dad an out.

Wayne held up a hand to stop him. "No, no, it's not okay. I was a foolish man back in the day and I'm ready to own up to the fact I did you wrong. I know it doesn't make it right, but things were different back then. I was different. I didn't want people talking and saying how my son was peculiar."

"We've been through this before. You said you didn't want people to talk about me like they did crazy Uncle Marvin," Jerry said, leaving out the point he'd recently learned his uncle wasn't so crazy after all.

"I know what I said, but thinking upon it some more, I realized that isn't the whole of it. It wasn't all about you. You can hate me if you want, but the truth of the matter was I didn't want them to think maybe I was as loony as the rest of the family."

"It's okay, Dad. Believe it or not, I understand."

Wayne chuckled, but the humor didn't reach his eyes. "The irony is, now that I'm ready to shout to the world and tell everyone what MY boy can do, I'm not allowed to say anything."

Of course there were those who did know, as the last time Jerry had visited, his father had gotten a little too carried away with the telling. Jerry decided it best not to mention the man's past indiscretions.

"How about we compromise?"

Wayne turned to face him. "How do we do that?"

"It's okay to let people know I'm your son, but we'll save the other stuff for a need-to-know basis."

"What if someone wants to know what you do for a living?"

"Tell them the truth – that I work for the government."

"What if they want to know more? Old people can be pretty nosey, you know."

Jerry smiled. "You know, I think you just hit the nail on the head."

Wayne frowned. "Meaning?"

"Use your age. If they press the issue, tell them you have more important things to remember than what your son does for a living."

Wayne grinned. "I can do that."

"I know you can, Pop. And, Pop."

"Yeah, son?"

"No one is to know anything about what April and Max can do."

Wayne's frown deepened. "What can they do?" Before Jerry could answer, his father winked.

Gunter woofed his approval as Jerry reached out a hand to help his dad out of the SUV.

Chapter Ten

Jerry followed his father into the house. He lowered the suitcases and stopped to admire the openness of the vaulted space and wall of windows that flooded the room with light and exposed the pool, which was surrounded by an outdoor living space and enclosed with a large screen. "That screen would come in handy against Michigan's mosquitos."

"It's called a birdcage. They are quite popular here in Florida." Wayne chuckled. "That didn't take long."

Jerry followed his glance as Max swam into view. Houdini trailed after her, pacing the concrete as she turned to make another lap. "You'll have a hard time getting her out of there."

"How long do you think it'll be before that dog

joins her?"

Houdini crouched as if debating jumping in, then pushed off, following her once more. Jerry gave a nod to Gunter. "I think he'll calm down as soon as he figures out Max is not in danger."

Gunter took the hint, pressing through the glass door to help settle the young dog.

"The only thing she's in danger of is seeing your mother get a cramp," Wayne said, speaking of Lori, who sat stiff as a board perched on the edge of her chair, watching Max's every move. "Perhaps you should tell the dog your mom is an avid swimmer and won't let anything happen to her granddaughter."

"Maybe it would be better if I tell Mom to relax. I can assure you that the dog will make it to Max before Mom even reaches the pool."

"You go make sure April is finding everything she needs. I'll go sit with them," Wayne said, waving him off. "We put you in the guest room down that hall since it is away from the others. It doesn't have its own bath, but there's one across the hall."

April sat on the bed, wearing nothing but a towel as she pulled a brush through her damp hair. She looked at the suitcase and smiled a sheepish grin. "I was so eager to take a shower, I was already naked before I stopped to realize I hadn't brought in anything to change into."

Jerry lifted the suitcase to the wooden luggage

rack sitting inside the closet. "Max didn't seem to have any trouble finding her bathing suit. She's already in the pool."

"It must have been in her backpack." April brushed past him as he stepped away from the closet.

She smelled so fresh. He lifted her hair and kissed the back of her neck.

April giggled and ducked out of the way. "Jerry, this is your parents' house. They'll hear."

"All I did was kiss your neck."

April arched an eyebrow. "That's the way it always starts."

"Then stop giggling." Taking a step, he looped a finger in the towel, watching as it fell to the ground. "Besides, my parents are outside with Max."

"Jerry?" Lori's voice floated through the closed door. "Do you need anything?"

April gasped.

"No, Mom, we're good."

"If you need anything, I'll be in the Kitchen. Max is hungry, so I'm going to start lunch. Don't worry. Wayne is watching her."

"The kitchen is on the other side of that wall," April whispered.

Jerry stooped to pick up the towel.

"Where are you going?"

"To take a shower." Jerry looked her over once more and sighed. "A very cold one."

***

Jerry opened his eyes and blinked several times. Sitting up on the bed, he lifted the throw blanket and saw he was still wearing the bath towel. He had a vague memory of coming out of the shower and seeing the bed, thinking he'd close his eyes for just a moment. Looking at the clock on the dresser, he realized that moment was four hours ago. He walked to the closet to get his clothes from his suitcase and saw his and April's clothes hanging on the bar. The suitcases were all sitting at the bottom of the closet with the suitcase rack folded and tucked behind. He moved to the dresser and found a drawer with his socks and underwear. His stomach grumbled as he dressed, reminding him of his mother's promise of lunch. He opened the bedroom door. The house was quiet. Too quiet.

He went to the living room and looked out at the pool. Empty.

He plodded across the tile floor to check the driveway and saw the Durango still parked where he'd left it. He went to the garage. While his parents' Chrysler was still there, both golf carts were missing, which meant he'd slept through the raising of the garage door.

"I must have been more tired than I thought." He shut the inner door and went to the kitchen in search of food. He found a note along with his cell phone and a bottle opener on the kitchen island: *Jerry, you were sleeping so soundly, I didn't want to wake you.*

There is a sandwich in the fridge and snacks in the cabinet. Your parents are giving us a tour of The Villages. PS, I love this kitchen. Is it too late to add a tiered island to my wish list?

Jerry took in the island that wrapped around the kitchen and helped cordon off the room from the open living and dining space. The added tier proved useful for hiding the sink and allowing a buffer for those sitting at one of the eight barstools that lined it. Jerry stepped back and snapped several photos, which he sent to Dan along with a note instructing the builder to add it to their wish list. Pocketing the phone, he moved to the fridge and pulled out a plate with a heavily stacked turkey sandwich. He remembered the bottle opener and returned to the refrigerator. Moving aside the pitcher of what he knew to be sweet tea, he saw a six-pack of Budweiser. Jerry smiled and pulled one free. Opening the bottle, he sat at the counter, took a long drink and sighed. Though he was alone in the house, he could feel the warmth of spirits around him, and in this moment, he was utterly content.

The unmistakable ticking of nails on the tile drew his attention. Jerry looked to see Gunter staring at him.

Gunter wagged his tail.

"I'm glad to see you too, boy."

Instead of approaching, Gunter cut through the opening and looked toward the far counter. Placing his front legs on the counter, the dog looked back at Jerry and licked his lips.

Jerry chuckled. "Something tells me there are cookies in the container."

Gunter woofed and licked his lips once more.

"Patience, my friend. When I'm finished with my lunch, we'll both have one."

This seemed to appease the ghostly K-9, who lowered to a crouch on the floor in front of the counter, guarding the cookies.

"Do you miss it?" Granny asked.

Jerry focused on the voice. As he did, his grandmother's spirit materialized in front of the fridge.

Gunter rose to greet her.

"Miss what?" Jerry asked.

"The days when it was just you and Gunter."

"No."

"That was a quick answer. You didn't even take a moment to think about it."

"There's nothing to think about. I am a happy man."

"I know. I just like hearing it." Granny opened the fridge and retrieved the pitcher of tea. Removing the lid, she dipped her finger into the liquid, then put it in her mouth and wrinkled her nose. Moving to the counter, she added more sugar before tasting it once more. "Much better."

"You're going to give them diabetes," Jerry said

as she poured a glass.

Granny added a few ice cubes, dipped her hand through the container of cookies and tossed Gunter a cookie before rounding the counter and climbing onto the tall barstool next to him. "I put a little bug in Max's ear."

"You're not talking about a real bug, are you?"

Granny cackled. "Of course not. I just told her I think she and her mom should stay here while you and Gunter take care of your business."

While he didn't have a problem leaving them here, he wondered at the reasoning. "Care to tell me why?"

"It will be good for her."

Jerry nodded his agreement. "I like that Max is getting to know her grandparents."

"I agree, but that wasn't the 'her' I was referring to."

"Oh?"

"I watched April at lunch. Once she overcame the nervousness of meeting Lori and Wayne, the joy on her face was palpable."

"Really?"

"Yes. I think it would be good for her to spend some time alone with them. Max too."

"Okay, I'll make the suggestion when they get back."

Granny took a sip of her tea. "No, let them bring it to you."

"Why?"

"So April doesn't feel as though you are forcing her to have a relationship with your parents."

"I thought you said…"

Granny placed a hand on his knee.

That was the way with his grandmother. Even when alive, she had a way about her that let him know when to push back and when to give in to her requests. "Yes, ma'am."

Gunter barked and ran down the hall, disappearing through the door that led to the garage.

A moment later, the door opened. April broke into a huge smile the moment she saw him. "Feel better?"

"It definitely took the edge off. I didn't mean to crash. I just thought to close my eyes for a moment."

"Stop apologizing." April draped her arms around his neck and kissed him. "We all understand."

The door opened. April released him as Houdini came inside, just in front of Max and his parents. Max saw him, held up a paintbrush, and grinned. "Grandma and I are going to paint my room."

Jerry looked at Lori. "Grandma?"

Lori beamed. "It appears Granny is already taken."

Wayne dipped and gave Lori a kiss on the cheek. "You're too young to be a granny anyway."

"What's wrong with the pink?" They all turned

to look at him. "What am I missing?"

Wayne chuckled. "Have you seen the room?"

Max winced. "It's really pink."

"Max, you should be grateful."

His mother waved him off. "No, it is I who am grateful that Max had enough courage to tell me what she thought. I knew it was awful. So did your father. He wouldn't let me see it until he was finished painting it. He opened the door to show me, and it took my breath away. I asked if it was too pink, and he said it was too late. I thought I could tone it down with bedding, but then I just kept adding to it and making it worse."

"What color are you going to go with?"

"We're keeping the pink. We're going to tone it by adding thick white stripes." Lori smiled at April. "It was April's idea. She really has a knack for decorating."

April's cheeks pinkened under the compliment. "I've spent a lot of time on Pinterest looking for ideas for the house. Speaking of which, did you get my note?"

"I've already sent Dan the pictures," Jerry assured her.

"It's too bad you live in Michigan. I sure could use April's help getting this place updated."

Jerry was about to ask what needed to be updated, when April spoke up. "I don't mind staying here while Jerry sees to things." She searched his face as if checking to ensure she hadn't overstepped.

"Oh, that would be wonderful." Lori's tone echoed April's enthusiasm. "We would love to have April and Max stay with us for as long as it takes."

Jerry had to hand it to his grandmother. The woman had a way of getting things done in short order. Recalling what she'd said about making April think it was her idea, he kept his reply lowkey. "If you want to stay and help out, that is fine with me."

***

"Are you sure you don't mind my staying?" He searched April's face for any sign of hesitation.

"I'm sure," Jerry told her for the sixth time. "Although I really don't see anything that needs to be changed."

April laughed. "That's because you're a guy. Your mom just moved into someone else's house. Of course, there'll be things she wants to change to make it her own."

"How does having you help make it her own?"

"Are you asking that because you don't want me to stay?"

"No, I'm asking it because I'm a guy, and being one, I don't know how all of this works."

"You've remodeled before," she reminded him. "Don't you remember how it felt when you were done and you knew you'd accomplished something?"

"Yes, but when I remodeled, it was because the

place was hideous."

April cocked an eyebrow. "You don't see anything hideous about the television the size of a piece of plywood on the far wall?"

Jerry swallowed. "You're saying I should scratch that off my wish list?"

April giggled. "We'll discuss that once we have walls."

Jerry pumped his fist into the air.

"What was that for?"

"For telling me there was still a chance."

April shook her head. "You're such a guy."

"Yep, so is my dad, and I happen to know that television is probably what sold him on the house."

April blew out a sigh. "Fine, the television monstrosity can stay."

"You're not mad?"

"Of course not. I'm pretty sure Max and I will be spending most of our time lying around the pool working on our tans."

Jerry smiled. "That girl is going to be in the pool more than she'll be out of it."

"She's like a fish," April agreed. "Listen, I know I had misgivings at first, but your parents are great. Go do what you do and earn some of that money the company pays you."

"If you need me…"

"Jerry, you're leaving us with your parents. We're in The Villages. What could possibly go wrong?"

Gunter groaned.

Bunny appeared in front of them, shaking her head. "Uh oh."

"She really needs to stop tempting fate like that," Granny agreed.

April sighed and spoke to those she could not see. "I'm not tempting fate. I am being practical."

"They may be right," Jerry said. "Maybe I should have Gunter stay here."

"You'll do no such thing. Gunter goes where you go, and that's final. If I leave the house, I'll be with one of your parents. Your dad said something about playing golf. If Max leaves the house, Houdini will be with her." April frowned. "You don't have a bad feeling about leaving, do you?"

"No." It was the truth.

"Did Max tell you she had a bad feeling when you told her goodbye?"

"No."

"Good, then get out of here. You're on company time. Now go."

"Yes, ma'am." Jerry kissed her firmly on the lips, then turned to leave. Hesitating at the door, he gave her a long look. "Love you, Ladybug."

April smiled. "Love you too, McNeal."

Chapter Eleven

Jerry plugged the directions into the navigator and looked over at Gunter. "You sure you don't want to stay with the girls?"

Gunter gave a soft growl and looked at him as if to say, *You're not getting rid of me that easily.*

"Okay, but just so you know, Mom said something about making more cookies with Max."

Gunter licked his lips.

Jerry laughed and roughed the dog's fur. "Don't worry, boy. I'm sure she'll save you some."

Gunter answered with a single woof and settled into the passenger seat.

While Jerry loved traveling with April and Max, he enjoyed the ease of traveling with Gunter. Since the dog was a spirit, there was no talking when he needed to concentrate and no need to stop at every rest area. They'd been on the road for just over an hour when Gunter, who'd been lying in the seat with his head on the console, sat up and sniffed the air. The dog's ears pinged like a subtle radar, looking and listening for the threat.

Jerry's spidey senses tingled. Though he knew the threat was near, a sense of contentedness filled him. "Like Batman and Robin, Starsky and Hutch, Tonto and the Lone Ranger, Jerry and Gunter are back at it, fighting crime."

Gunter barked an enthusiastic bark.

Jerry chuckled. "That's what I like about you, dog. You get my humor."

A panel truck loomed in the distance. Instantly, Jerry knew that was the source of the threat. He looked at Gunter. "What do you think? Is that our guy?"

Gunter growled.

"Yeah, I thought so." Jerry moved closer. Seemingly not in any hurry, the driver had his left leg outside the open door, using the driver's side mirror as a foot prop. Cutting into the right lane far enough back to avoid suspicion, Jerry pressed the button to call Fred.

"McNeal?"

"I need you to run a plate."

"You know you have that fancy computer attached to the dash for precisely that reason."

Jerry glanced at the computer, which he

had barely used. "You know that's more April's line of work than mine."

Fred chuckled. "Living with that grandmother of yours has kept you in the dark ages."

"Better watch your tone, or I'll see to it she haunts you." The fact that Fred didn't have an immediate comeback let him know his boss was weighing the possibilities.

"What's the plate?" Fred asked after a moment.

Jerry rattled off the number.

"Got it. Now tell me what you've got."

"Nothing other than the driver is stupid and my gut telling me this guy needs to be stopped."

"The plate is clean. Let me see what we can get on the driver."

"Presuming the truck is registered to him," Jerry added.

"You think that might not be the case?"

Jerry sighed. "Unfortunately, that's exactly what I'm getting."

"You have authorization to stop him if that's the way you want to play it."

A chill ran the length of Jerry's spine. "No. Not without backup. The man's looking for a fight."

"He's driving aggressively?"

"No, he's driving like a Sunday driver. Listen, don't ask me to explain it. Just get me some help."

"It's already on the way. Just sit tight."

"Will do." Jerry followed behind the man for

several miles. Then as if discovering he was there, the driver pulled in his foot and angled the mirror to see him better.

Jerry glanced at Gunter. "We're blown."

Gunter woofed his agreement.

Jerry played several scenarios in his head before pulling to the shoulder.

Gunter grumbled his discontent.

"Don't worry; he isn't going to get away. The guy spotted us, but my gut tells me he wasn't sure if we were a threat. By pulling to the side, we took away his reason to bolt." Jerry pulled back onto the road, keeping his distance so as not to further spook the man. Traffic grew heavy just as the landscape changed from open fields to trees. Not wishing to lose sight of the suspect, Jerry inched closer.

Even before Jerry saw the blue lights of a police cruiser on the opposite side of the road, the panel truck veered to the shoulder. "Yo, dude, way to admit guilt."

The guy was out even before the wheels stopped. Jerry saw the rifle in the man's hand and swore under his breath as he got an image of a cluster of houses on the other side of the woods. Jerry switched on his overhead lights and pulled to the side of the road as the man disappeared into the trees. He pushed the emergency button on the overhead console, which was a direct line to Fred.

"McNeal?"

"Our guy just bailed. Gunter and I are going after him. Backup will be here in two minutes. Tell the officer not to shoot me," Jerry said as the police cruiser made a U-turn across the center median.

"Roger that."

Gunter led the way through the woods, and for a moment, Jerry wished he'd brought Houdini as well, a thought that left as soon as it came to him. Houdini and Max were a team, and she'd have eagerly followed after him. Pushing the thought away, he continued to search for the man.

The brush grew thicker. Jerry looked for Gunter, didn't see him, then saw a path of freshly trampled brush. Jerry followed. He heard movement behind him but wasn't concerned. The threat was in front of him and getting closer with each step. He pushed through the branches, saw the man standing there, and raised his pistol. The man didn't move. "Son of a ..."

Jerry lowered his gun once more and walked to where he'd seen the man. He snatched the discarded shirt from the branch where it had been left to distract him. He pivoted, scanning the shadows in search of the man. Seeing nothing, he continued, moving forward and to the danger he knew was to come. A child flashed into his mind. A boy who looked to be eight or nine, playing in a fenced yard just beyond the trees. Another image, this one of a man who was already dead. *He's killed once. He'll do it again.*

There was no time for stealth; he needed to distract the guy before he got to the child. *Gunter, take me to him before it's too late.*

Gunter pressed through the brush, circled, then ran off, leaving Jerry to follow. They were close. The child was close. He saw the fence. The child. The gun.

Jerry yelled without seeing, screaming for the suspect to stop and stepped into the clearing just as the suspect turned the barrel away from the child and pointed it in his direction. Jerry couldn't chance the shot since the boy was standing directly behind the guy, negating a clean shot. The police officer came up behind him. Jerry resigned himself to his fate. It was okay. The police officer would take the man down before he had a chance to turn his weapon on the boy. As Jerry braced for the bullet, he sent out a mental cry for help.

Three shots rang out.

Both man and boy dropped to the ground.

A branch cracked as the police officer stepped up beside him.

Jerry breathed a sigh of relief as the boy slowly picked himself off the ground.

The officer swore under his breath and something about it being a miracle.

***

Traffic diverted to the other lane; a slow stream

of vehicles inched by, and the passengers craned their necks to see what was holding them up. Some wielded cell phones, hoping to capture the perfect shot. To their disappointment, all they would see was Jerry leaning against his Durango, recounting his story for the tenth time, this time to Sergeant Bricker, the on-scene supervisor who'd just arrived. He knew exactly what to say as he'd listened when Officer Smith relayed the events to the second officer, who had arrived on the scene only moments after Smith had subdued the suspect. While Officer Smith had shown remorse for having shot the man, there was a mingling of excitement and awe in his voice when he'd gotten to the part of the actual takedown.

Sergeant Bricker stood, feet parted with a notebook in hand, waiting for Jerry to continue. "You yelled for the suspect to stop, and he aimed his rifle at you. You had a weapon. Why didn't you use it?"

"I didn't have a clean shot. There was a boy on the other side of the fence. He must have heard me yell and climbed on the fence to see what was going on."

"You were afraid you would hit the boy?"

"I couldn't take the chance."

"In your opinion, should Officer Smith have taken the shot?"

"The boy dropped as soon as the suspect fired at

me. Smith had a clean shot, and he took it."

"Smith called it a miracle that you weren't hit," Bricker said. "Do you agree?"

"If by miracle, you mean divine intervention, then yes."

"Isn't it possible the guy was just a lousy shot?"

"Nope."

"You sound pretty sure."

"The man was a killer on a mission. He'd already killed at least one person. He would have killed that boy and many more if Smith hadn't taken him down."

"How can you be so sure?"

"It's my job to be sure."

"Is that why you didn't wait for backup before following the man into the woods?"

Jerry started to tell him of his vision but knew it would only bring up more questions. "I acted on instinct. If we lost the man, we would have had to wait for the dogs."

"Smith said you led him straight to the suspect." The supervisor peered at Jerry. "Those are some serious tracking skills you've got."

"Boy Scouts." Jerry offered the barest of smiles when Gunter growled a grumbling growl.

An officer who'd been searching the panel truck approached and handed the sergeant a clipboard. "Our suspect's name is Kyle Drumond."

Glancing at the paper, the sergeant's face paled.

Lifting the paper, he swore under his breath and passed the clipboard to Jerry.

Jerry looked at the paper, which turned out to be a detailed map of a hospital, with hard targets and escape routes. The second sheet of paper had a list of additional names and targets. The first two names on the list were already lined out.

"I guess that hunch of yours was right," Bricker said when Jerry returned the clipboard.

"Does that mean I'm free to go?" The look that followed told Jerry everything he needed to know. Fred had already been in contact and had seen he wouldn't be detained.

Bricker pulled out his cell phone. "I'll call Mr. Jefferies with an update."

***

Jerry swiped to answer Fred's call.

Fred's voice boomed through the speakers. "You want to tell me what happened out there?"

Jerry looked at Gunter. "I guess the boss didn't believe the report."

Fred ignored the quip as he relayed Smith's statement. "I heard Mr. McNeal yell and knew I was close. As I stepped into the clearing, I saw the suspect raise his weapon. McNeal wasn't in a position to shoot without hitting the kid. Neither was I, but I raised my weapon anyway, figuring the boy would get scared and drop as soon as he saw the suspect shoot McNeal. I didn't really count on the guy missing McNeal since he had him dead to rights. Either it was a miracle or our suspect hadn't fired the gun before and wasn't aware of the kick. Anyway, that kid dropped like a lead balloon the second he heard the shot. I fired two rounds and dropped the man where he stood."

"That's what the man said," Jerry agreed.

"I know what the man said happened. What I want to know is the Jerry McNeal version and not the Boy Scout version you regurgitated for Bricker."

Jerry looked at Gunter once more. "I think the boss is onto us."

Gunter smiled a K-9 grin.

"It wasn't a miracle. It was divine intervention. Gunter led me straight to the guy. I knew he'd already killed and knew he wouldn't hesitate to kill the boy."

"You knew?"

"Saw it in my mind's eye. That's why I went after the guy. I wasn't being reckless. I saw the boy in the yard and knew Drumond would kill him and then go on to kill others."

"And you were prepared to die to keep that from happening?"

"Seemed like a good plan at the moment."

"Go on."

"I asked for help, and it showed up."

"By help, I take it you mean ghosts."

"Spirit," Jerry corrected. "Just one."

Gunter growled a low growl.

"Sorry, two, counting Gunter. As Drumond pulled the trigger, Tisdale grabbed the gun barrel, throwing off the shot. At the same time, Gunter sacked the kid, knocking him to the ground and allowing Smith to make a clean shot."

"Smith didn't see any of this?"

"It's hard to say. Sometimes, when the energy is that intense, spirits can be seen."

"But he didn't say he saw anything?"

"I guess it's easier to believe in miracles than divine intervention."

"Aren't they the same thing?"

"Sometimes."

"Too bad you didn't have Houdini with you," Fred said after a moment. "It may have been a little easier sell if they would have seen the dog."

Gunter yawned.

Instantly, an image of Max came to mind, and a chill washed over him. "Houdini is only half ghost, and Max and him are a team."

Fred caught the implication. "You're a lucky man, McNeal."

"That I am," Jerry agreed.

"I'll get Sinclair a message and let him know you'll be there soon." Fred ended the call without waiting for Jerry to acknowledge the comment.

A tingle crept over him. Jerry looked in the mirror and saw Granny sitting in the middle-row seat.

"Mr. Jefferies is such a nice man."

Jerry checked the road then glanced at his grandmother once more. "You knew this was going to happen. That's why you didn't want April and Max coming along."

Granny nodded. "Max would have insisted on using Houdini to track the man. Gunter can withstand things, Houdini can't."

Jerry nodded his understanding.

"You're learning, Jerry."

"Learning what?"

"Not to be specific. If you had asked Gunter to help, he would have helped you, and Lord knows where that would have left the boy. If you had asked me, I wouldn't have known to lift the gun barrel. By simply asking for help and leaving your request open-ended, you were able to save them all."

"I was scared."

Granny laughed. "Of course you were, Jerry. You're only human after all."

Chapter Twelve

Max had finally tired enough of the pool that Lori was able to convince her to join her in making cookies. Wayne was off golfing with his buddies, meaning April had the pool all to herself. While the air was a bit muggy, the breeze drifting in through the covered courtyard was delightful as the six-foot stucco wall that surrounded the outdoor area offered plenty of privacy. She floated on the raft, taking in the brilliant blue skies and watching as the occasional cloud floating past cast a shadow over the pool as the air conditioning cycled on and off. Other than that, the hum of a lawnmower way off in the distance and the occasional backup alarm from a golf cart were the only sounds disturbing her otherwise peaceful oasis.

The birdcage kept away the bugs, though the

occasional lizard would climb the screen. April didn't mind, as she enjoyed watching them, and she couldn't recall when she'd been more relaxed. Suddenly glad Jerry had agreed to Max's request for a pool, she sighed. "I could so get used to this." She closed her eyes.

Sometime later, the glass door slid open. Houdini's eager yips filled the air, shattering the silence. The area in between the birdcage and stucco fence wall held a small, narrow storage closet, the equipment for the saltwater pool, and was otherwise set up as a dog run for the previous owner's dog. With the exception of a six-by-six grassy area near the southern front of the house, the outer area was paved with small, round pebbles. Houdini considered this space his personal playground and wasted no time pushing his way through the doggy door built into the outer door. Lowering his nose to the ground, he ran back and forth in the graveled run.

"He kept whining. Grandma thinks he needs to do his business, but I think he just wants to chase the lizards. Do you want me to stay out here with him?"

"No, keep doing what you're doing, I'll keep an eye on him."

Max stepped outside and looked about as if searching for something. "Are you okay out here, Mom? The air feels a little weird."

"It's called humidity."

Max walked through the outdoor living area and

peeked down the left side of the enclosed yard to check on Houdini. "Are you sure?"

April wasn't sure if Max was picking up on something or if she was being a mother hen. That her daughter hadn't warned her of anything specific gave the impression it was the latter. April felt a pang of guilt. *It's my fault. She needs to stop worrying about me and learn to be a kid.* "It's alright, Max. I'll keep an eye on Houdini. You go and have fun with your grandmother."

"Okay, Mom." Max opened the sliding door to oldies music blaring from inside. Max turned her head, whispering so only her mother could hear. "Grandma Lori listens to weird music."

April laughed. "I'm sure your grandchildren will say the same about you one day."

Max smiled and went inside, sliding the door shut behind her.

April peeked to make sure Houdini was behaving, then closed her eyes. A rock tinked off the saltwater tank. Another followed. April looked to see Houdini frantically digging in the stones. Using her hands to paddle, April moved to the far edge of the pool. "Houdini, leave it!"

The dog ignored her command.

April firmed her voice. "Houdini, leave it!"

Once again, Houdini ignored the command.

Ignoring commands wasn't like him. Sure, Max had assumed full responsibility for his training, but it had been months since he'd disobeyed a direct command from any of them. "Houdini, come!" April said, using her sternest tone.

Houdini paused what he was doing, whined his displeasure, then raced through the pebbles, pushed through the flap, and stood looking down at her from the side of the pool.

"Good boy," April cooed.

Houdini wagged his tail.

"Lie down."

The tail stilled, but the dog continued to stand.

April narrowed her eyes. "Don't think that just because I'm in the pool, you don't have to listen. Now, lie down." She added the accompanying hand signal for good measure.

Houdini lowered to the concrete.

"Good boy," April said once more. Feeling triumphant, she rolled onto her back and closed her eyes. Moments later, a pebble pinged against the saltwater tank. April turned to see Houdini furiously digging in the same spot. "Why, you little stink butt!"

"Perhaps the dog has found something better to do than watch you sunbathe."

April rolled off the raft, using the flimsy plastic as a shield as she rotated in the pool, searching for the body behind the voice. "Who's there?"

Nothing.

The voice was male, of that she was certain.

Perhaps someone standing on the other side of the wall. No, distracted or not, Houdini would have alerted if anyone was there.

"Houdini, leave it."

"Let him dig. It will give us time to talk."

April turned toward the voice but saw no one. A shiver ran through her even though she wasn't cold. *Maybe I should call for Gunter. Easy, April, you don't want to scare Jerry. Think. What would Jerry do? Well, for one thing, he wouldn't let the spirit know he'd rattled him. Wait? Jerry says Gunter always wears his vest if he senses a threat. Houdini hasn't even acknowledged the spirit. That must mean he doesn't see him as a threat.* April let out a long breath to steady herself as she swam to the steps and exited the pool. Wrapping a towel around herself, she walked to the covered living area and sat with her back to the wall. "You want to talk, talk," she said more calmly than she felt.

"I'm looking for my wife."

Wife? Instantly, April recalled the spirit she'd been speaking to in Pennsylvania. "Mr. Bigsby? What can I do for you?"

"It's about time. I need you to talk to my wife."

Wait, that's not the same voice.

"I was here first."

"Too bad, she called me by name," Bigsby said heatedly.

Great, my first solo run and I've already made a

mess of things. Okay, April, you started this, you need to fix it. "Mr. Bigsby, I'm sorry. I will help you, but now isn't the time."

"Then why did you call for me?"

"I thought you were already here. Please. I'm sorry, but you really need to leave. Hello?" April said when he didn't answer.

"He's gone."

April recognized the voice as belonging to the original spirit. "Please tell me your name so I know who I'm talking to."

"Harold."

"Harold? Like in Carol and Harold?"

"The same."

"I'm sorry you died."

"Not sorry enough to steal this house."

Wait, what?! "I didn't steal this house; I don't even live here."

"Then what are you doing in my pool?"

April gulped. "This is my fiancé's parents' house. Carol sold it to Wayne and Lori. Jerry and I are here visiting."

"The McNeals bought my house?"

"Yes."

"They are good people."

"You know them?"

"Of course. We all used to play cards together."

"So you're not mad?"

"Only at myself. Carol wouldn't have had to

move if I would have told her."

"Told her what? I can help if you let me," April said when the spirit failed to answer.

"How do I know I can trust you?"

Good question. "I can cross my heart."

"How about I just promise to make your life miserable if you don't keep up your end of the bargain?"

April gulped. "I guess that works too."

"Carol shouldn't have moved. She loved this house."

"Don't take this the wrong way, but it's just a house. Maybe it was just too painful to live here without you."

"I have to go. Tell Carol I love her and I left a little treasure for her."

"Wait? Is it something in the house?" There was no response.

A rock tinked.

Needing to lash out at something, April focused her frustration on the dog. "Houdini, stop dig…" April stopped mid-sentence. "That's why Harold insisted Houdini keep digging. He's found the treasure."

Chapter Thirteen

There was nothing tying Sinclair's mid-century sprawling brick ranch to Florida. In fact, it would have looked at home in about any state, including Michigan. The palm tree landscape, on the other hand, was quintessential Florida, as were the tiny lizards that raced away whenever anyone neared. While Houdini had been enamored with the creatures since their arrival, Gunter couldn't be bothered. The same couldn't be said for the ebony German Shepherd who now clung to Sinclair's side and growled at him, as if doing so would prevent the dog from having his way with her.

"Easy, Maggie." Sinclair shrugged his apologies when the dog continued to growl. "She's been extra protective of late."

It wasn't helping that Gunter was inching

forward, sniffing the air. "She's not in heat by chance, is she?"

"Yes. You know your dogs."

More like he knew Gunter's fondness for female shepherds. Jerry sighed. Having Gunter keen on keeping his lineage going was one thing; knocking up Sinclair's shepherd would be bad news all the way around. So far, Jerry had Fred convinced Houdini was a fluke. If his boss were to get wind of it being a regular occurrence, he would insist on finding a way to literally spread the love. *Gunter, back off before I call Granny to come put a leash on you.*

Realizing Jerry was serious, Gunter tucked his tail and returned to his side.

"Good girl," Sinclair said when Maggie eased her stance. He moved aside so Jerry could enter, then closed the door and led the way to the kitchen. "Coffee? I just made a fresh pot."

Jerry smiled. "I'd love a cup."

"Fred said you had quite the adventure on the way here. Normally, they'd call in the dogs to do the search. That dog of yours would have no trouble following that trail."

For a moment, Jerry thought the man was talking about Gunter, then realized he was referring to Houdini. Since Fred told him he'd read Sinclair in, there was no reason to keep Gunter a secret. "The report will say I was good at tracking. The truth of the matter is Gunter led me to him."

"Gunter? That's the invisible dog?"

"He's not invisible. He's a spirit."

"Is he here?"

Jerry knew where this was going. "He is."

"Is he in this room?"

Jerry looked to where Gunter was crouched on the cool tile floor, watching Maggie's every move. "He is."

"I can't see him. Therefore, I stand by my assessment."

"Why am I here, Mr. Sinclair?"

"Because Mr. Jefferies sent you."

Jerry expected Sinclair to laugh at his own joke, but there was no humor in the man's face. "You didn't ask him to send me?"

"I asked him about you. I told him I thought you to be a rather peculiar man who seemed to think you are haunted by the ghost of a dog."

Jerry bristled at being called peculiar by a man who fit that very description. "And he said?"

"Something about the pot calling the kettle black and told me if I ever found myself in need of an exorcist, you are the man."

Jerry nearly choked on his coffee. "If you expect me to perform an exorcism, I'm afraid you're out of luck."

"But you can see spirits?"

"I believe we've already established that."

"Good, then I need you to tell the ghost to leave."

Jerry sat back in the chair and crossed his arms. "I hate to break it to you, but I'm not seeing any spirits around you."

"That's because I told him he is not wanted. That is how it works, is it not?"

Jerry recalled his recent bid for solitude from the spirits and the grief he'd suffered. Still, his case was slightly different. "Sometimes."

"I thought so, and that is precisely what I did. I tried to get Josephine, that's my wife, to do the same, but she seems to think doing so is silly."

He looked at Gunter, who was rather amorous despite the fact he was a spirit. "Mr. Sinclair, you refer to your spirit as a male. He and your wife haven't…"

Sinclair nearly knocked over his coffee mug. "Great gracious, man, of course not. How is a thing like that even possible?"

"It's not." At least, he didn't think so. Then again, Gunter had… "How about you start from the beginning?"

"What beginning?"

"When did you and your wife first see this spirit?"

"I have not seen him."

"You said—"

"No, I said I told him to go away. I never said I saw him."

Jerry looked around the room in search of a camera. "Do you, by chance, know a woman by the name of Bunny Emerson?"

"No, should I?"

"No. I was just asking. When did your wife first see the spirit?"

"Josephine hasn't seen him either." Sinclair held up a hand. "My wife thinks this all an elaborate farce. It is our daughter, Emily, who has seen him. She told us about him after seeing him following my wife. Since then, she's mentioned seeing him multiple times. Out near the kennel."

"How long ago."

"A few months now."

"You didn't say anything when I told you about your daughter."

"I didn't believe you. At least, I didn't want to. Up until then, I just thought Emily was making things up. You know, like having an imaginary friend."

Jerry started to tell him that most imaginary friends were spirits and not actually figments of their imagination, but decided not to give him anything more to worry about. "Has your daughter spoken with him?"

"Not to my knowledge. I think she was just curious about him at first. Then she told me the man frightens her."

"Has he tried to hurt her?"

"No, but she said he comes around when she helps train the dogs, so she doesn't like doing that anymore. That's the main reason I told Mr. Jefferies I wanted to speak with you. My daughter is young, and she always enjoyed helping with the dogs. I don't know, I guess I thought she'd grow up following in my footsteps. Please promise me you can help."

"I can't."

Sinclair heaved a heavy sigh.

"No, I mean, I will try, but I can't make any promises until I see what it is that is keeping him here. I can't do that until he shows himself."

"How long will that take?"

That was the sticking point; there was no way to tell how long it would take. That the spirit hadn't already made himself known wasn't a good sign. "How about we start by you introducing me to your wife."

"She's not here. I suggested that both she and Emily go visit Josephine's sister in Melbourne as soon as I heard you were coming. That won't be a problem, will it? I can ask her to come home if you need her here." Sinclair fidgeted in his seat. "It's just that she is a nonbeliever and already thinks I'm making too much of this. If she finds out I brought in an expert and then tell her the spirit is gone without proof..."

Jerry nodded his understanding. "There is no

reason to tell your wife, not yet anyway. While it is possible the spirit has attached itself to your wife, I'm not getting the feeling that is the case. Would you mind if I check out the house?"

"Check it out?"

Gunter groaned.

Maggie's lip curled into a snarl.

Sinclair looked at his dog. "Is he here?"

"Your spirit is not here."

Sinclair stared at him without blinking. "My spirit."

"The spirit I came here to speak with," Jerry said, trying to appeal to the man's analytical mind. "Gunter moved, and that's what Maggie reacted to."

"Oh." Sinclair didn't sound convinced.

"Mr. Sinclair, how is it you are willing to bring me into your home to help you get rid of a ghost, but you are not willing to believe I travel with the spirit of a dog?"

"Well, when you put it that way."

"Can I walk through your home to see if I can see or feel any spirits?"

"You want me to walk with you?" Sinclair started to get up.

Jerry held up a hand to stop him. "It would be better if you don't. Keep Maggie here as well. Gunter and I will search the house and see what we find."

Sinclair frowned. "You're going to search my

house."

Talking to the man was like beating his head against the wall. Jerry worked to stay calm. "Gunter and I are going to do a quick walk through your house to see if we pick up anything – spirits. The invisible dog and I are going to walk through each room to check for spirits."

"Okay."

Gunter took the lead, weaving in and out of each room. While the dog stopped to sniff an occasional item, he keyed on nothing in particular. In the end, the house was just what it was – a nice, sprawling brick ranch home.

"Did you see him?" Sinclair asked when Jerry finished searching the home.

"Nope."

"It only took you five minutes. Search again. Maybe you missed him."

Jerry could understand the man's frustration. "It doesn't work that way. The spirit isn't here. Searching the house was just a formality to make sure. But honestly, if the spirit was in the house, I would have felt it even before I did the walk-through."

"So, you're giving up."

"No, I came here to help you."

"But you said…"

"I said the spirit wasn't in the house. I didn't say it wasn't hanging around the property. I didn't see any dogs other than Maggie, so I think it's safe to assume you don't train the dogs in the house."

"Oh, but I do. We do a number of searches here, digital forensic searches looking for thumb drives and hidden laptops. We also do some hide-and-seek games. The dogs love the hide-and-seek, as Emily has some great hiding spots. Josephine often helps her hide in the attic; you wouldn't think that's a thing, but criminals tend to think it is a good hiding place. Emily used to giggle a lot when we first started, but she's much better now. Sometimes, she falls asleep. That is the best because her breathing slows, and the dogs really have to work to find her."

"I saw your kennel out back when I pulled in. Let's you and I take a walk and see what we find."

Happy to be included, Sinclair sprang from the chair. Maggie woofed her readiness.

Gunter matched her eagerness with his own ghostly yaps.

Maggie stiffened.

"She must know we're heading to the kennels." Sinclair stretched his palm. "You're going to have to wait here, girl. She doesn't like the kennels much these days. We have twenty-two acres, including woods, a marsh with a stream, and a pond. We use every inch of it to train the dogs," Sinclair said as they exited the house.

Gunter lowered his nose and trotted ahead, leading the way to the kennel.

"Where do you get the dogs?"

"It depends. Some come from breeders. Others are rescued from the pounds. I have a team who helps train, plus I've gained some good contacts along the way. Sometimes, I'll get a call saying they have a dog I need to check out, then either I or someone from the team goes to see what's so special about that dog."

Sinclair stopped when they reached the kennel. "Is your friend dog-reactive?"

"My friend?"

"You know, your ghost dog."

Could it be Sinclair was coming around? Jerry watched as Gunter pressed through the door without waiting. "Gunter will be just fine."

"Good, on account of it's about to get loud," Sinclair said, then opened the heavy door to a frenzy of barking and whining. Gunter walked ahead, greeting each dog like a Gunny inspecting his troops. Some of the dogs took exception to the ghostly K-9's presence; others approached the gates with timid curiosity.

The building was pristine white and lined with well-maintained kennels on each side. Jerry did a quick count, noting twenty kennels, each enclosure large enough to house multiple dogs. Everything was painted a brilliant white, only offset by the grey polished floors. Instantly, he thought of his friend Mike, founder of Public Safety Dogs Inc., and how they were always in search of donations just to help feed and maintain the search and rescue dogs they trained to donate to law enforcement. "You must have some budget."

"I started this with family money," Sinclair said, moving into the room. "I'd been doing this about eight years when the agency brought me in. As I'm sure you know, the agency can be quite generous."

Jerry nodded his agreement. "Does your wife help with the training?"

"No. Not with the training."

"But she does help out."

"In other areas, yes. Why do you ask?"

"You said Emily doesn't like helping with the dogs anymore because the spirit scares her."

"That's right." Sinclair's eyes grew wide as he looked about the kennel. "You think the spirit is connected to the dogs?"

"It's too early to tell, but it's possible. Just so you know, I'm not picking up on anything just yet. Have you gotten any new dogs lately, and by 'lately,' I mean since your daughter started seeing the spirit?"

Sinclair shook his head. "No, these six came in about the same time. They are all between two and three years of age, and are all just about ready to head out. I have been working with them for nearly a year."

"Okay, so probably not attached to the dogs either."

Jerry watched as Gunter sprinted up a set of steps on the far end of the kennel. "What's upstairs?"

"Some trainer rooms. They are unoccupied at the moment."

"So, you train up there?"

"No, not training rooms, trainer rooms. A bunkhouse of sorts. It's for the handlers. You'd think it would be loud, but it's pretty well insulated. Besides, most of the people who stay here are used to the sound of dogs barking."

"And they stay there for how long?"

"Depends. You don't just train a dog and send them on their way into the great unknown. That would be a recipe for failure. The trainers come and work with the dogs for as long as it takes to become a team. Some stay for a few weeks, and others longer, often a month or more, to work with the dogs before they head out. Sometimes, a K-9 team comes in for refresher training, especially when some new training technique becomes available or if a dog or team needs a refresher."

"Any possibility one of them left something in one of the bunk rooms?"

"Nope."

"You seem sure."

"The rooms get professionally cleaned after each stay. Josephine double checks them after they're clean and again before each visit. Do you want to take a look?"

The fact that Gunter was now standing beside him let Jerry know there was no need. "No."

"Are you sure? The ghost might be up there."

If Jerry hadn't personally witnessed Emily's gift when Sinclair was testing Houdini, he might be inclined to question if the man even had an entity. "You said all the training is done here on the premises?"

"Most of it. The advanced training is more difficult because a lot of it is done off-site to allow for different sights and sounds. That's important because the dogs are used to being out here in the country, and we need to make sure they're ready to hit the pavement in the city if that is the agency they're placed with. We don't train at random. We know the job these dogs are headed for before they are even fully trained. Every now and then, a dog will surprise us and not be suited for that work. If that is the case, we'll change it up and train them for something else."

"What happens if they fail at that?"

Sinclair offered a rare laugh. "We can usually find something they are suited for. We had a beagle once that was supposed to sniff out bombs. Every time we turned around, he was leading us to bugs."

Jerry matched his chuckle. "That's useful."

"Actually, it is," Sinclair agreed. "The dog's making a name for himself, sniffing out bedbugs in luxury hotels."

"Nice." Jerry pointed at the dogs, most of which were focused on Gunter, who was sitting in the middle of the floor scratching an imaginary itch. "Tell me about them."

Sinclair walked the row, naming each dog and telling of their specialty. He pointed to a golden retriever. "Sadie has a terrific nose for sniffing out explosives. She'll be working with a handler in airport security. Her brother came in with her, but he flunked out several weeks into the program."

"Too rambunctious?"

"On the contrary, too docile. The dog moved at one speed."

"Where is he now?"

"Sent him to your neck of the woods. He's now living the good life in Rochester Hills, excelling at the top of his class on the Leaders for the Blind Campus."

"That's cool."

Sinclair smiled. "Isn't it, though?" Pointing to the kennel, he continued. "Teddy, the Australian shepherd, is agile enough to get through the rubble and is going to do a search and rescue. Those two shepherds, Murph and Kera, are going to the White House to welcome guests and sniff out contraband. The dogs are at the stage where they will start their advanced training. We've gone off-site with them before, but now the training gets more intense. We've got connections in the state, so we'll start piggybacking on real cases. We hear of a bust, and we'll take the dogs in to see if they can find what we already know is there. The same with Maggie; she's a cadaver dog, so she'll be going to real murder scenes and..."

Gunter barked, sending the rest of the kennel in a barking frenzy.

The hairs on the back of Jerry's neck stood on end.

"Wh...wha...what's happening?" Sinclair stammered.

"You said Maggie doesn't like the kennels much these days. When did that start?"

"A couple of months ago. She was fine until we got a fresh shipment of bones." The color drained from Sinclair's face as he realized the implication.

Chapter Fourteen

It took several moments for the color to return to Sinclair's face.

Being a patient man and not seeing a reason to rush things, Jerry waited for him to gather his composure.

"You think Maggie is haunted?" Sinclair said at last.

"No, but there's a very good chance the bones you received belong to someone who's rather unhappy with them being here."

"You're saying the dead guy wants his body back."

"Perhaps."

"But…"

"Let's not get ahead of ourselves. There is a good chance the guy may not know he's dead. Even if he does, he may not be pleased with the way his remains are being used."

"And if that's the case?"

"We might have to look at returning the skeleton for a proper burial."

Sinclair blinked his surprise. "You don't know how this works, do you?"

"I don't know everything, but I've got a pretty good handle on the spirit world."

"No, I mean cadaver dog training."

"Yes, you bury a body, and the dog finds it."

"Bones, McNeal. We bury bones. And teeth and hair and blood and tissue. They are not bodies; they are pieces of them. Teeth, gotten from a dentist. Hair collected from beauty salons, then washed and processed to remove all chemical residue. Blood, organs and tissue collected from…" Sinclair hesitated. "You get the drift."

"And the bones?"

Sinclair shrugged. "Mostly, I order them from the internet."

Now Jerry was the one staring. "You can do that?"

Sinclair nodded. "Google it. I assure you it's a thing."

Jerry rocked back on his heels. "I had no clue."

"The bottom line is I've got lots of body parts, but not all from one person. Even if I did, I would not be able to reconstruct the poor fellow. While the bones are intact, the other stuff isn't more than a scent. Perfect for training dogs, but nothing of use to anyone else, even if that person is deceased."

"Let's find the spirit, and then we'll try to reason with him."

"You can do that?"

"I can certainly try."

"Can I go with you?"

Jerry debated his answer. "Yes, if you can suspend your beliefs."

"Meaning I have to believe in ghosts?"

"Meaning if you see me talking to someone who isn't there, don't interrupt."

"Okay. Where are we going?" Sinclair asked when Jerry started for the door.

"To find your ghost." Now that Jerry had an idea of the problem, all he needed to do was follow the pull and Gunter, who now led the charge as they moved away from both the house and kennel building. The property was cordoned off in various training areas, some of which were simple, others elaborate structures that would test the dog's agility. They tramped through an area of tall brush which Jerry now knew to be a field of teeth and bones. He also knew they were not the bones they were looking for. He noticed an enclosed area of rubble off to the left, littered with cars, boards, and beams. The debris field was surrounded by what looked like thick plexiglass. "What's all of that?"

"That's where the dogs get their first brush with an active building search and rescue. We bring in volunteers who don't mind getting buried for a few hours and allow the dogs to find them."

"And the plexiglass?"

"We have a Jack Russell who can sniff out snakes, but it's hard to find volunteers willing to chance lying in a pile of fire ants."

"I can see where that would be a deterrent."

"It's easier to control the scene this way. After the dogs master this, we take them out into the real world."

Gunter ran ahead to check out a large agility playland.

Jerry watched in disbelief as his ghostly partner climbed the ladder with ease and then began a slow, tight walk to the other side.

Sinclair stopped and stared in Gunter's direction. He stuck his index finger in his mouth and held it up to the wind. "Huh."

For a moment, Jerry thought Sinclair could see him. "Huh, what?"

"The rope's swaying."

"And?"

"That rope is too heavy to move on its own. And the wind isn't strong enough to move it."

"It's moving because Gunter is walking across it."

"I thought you said he's a German shepherd."

"He is."

"Was he military trained?"

"Not that I'm aware of."

"Huh," Sinclair said once more.

"You keep saying that."

"That structure is set up for Malinois."

"Malinois. They're like German shepherds, right?"

"Jefferies said you were in the Marines."

"That's right."

"Is that something like being in the Navy?"

Jerry chuckled. "You've made your point."

"You're saying your dog just walked across it without falling?"

"Yep."

Sinclair nodded. "I guess this is one of those times I'm supposed to suspend my belief."

"I guess so," Jerry agreed. "Though I'd like to think seeing the rope move helped."

"It didn't hurt, that's for sure."

Gunter appeared in the clearing, barking to indicate he'd found something.

Jerry hurried ahead, stopping where the dog indicated. "There are bones buried here."

"How could you possibly know that?"

"You're a smart man, Sinclair. Figure it out."

The man's eyes grew wide. "Gunter?"

That Sinclair had called him by name said a lot. Jerry looked to where Gunter now stood, indicating yet another find. "There's another one about twenty feet from here," Jerry said, pointing to where they lay.

"I know where the bones are. I thought we were looking for the spirit."

"The spirit isn't with these bones."

"Meaning they aren't his?"

"I'm pretty sure this set belongs to your guy, but not the ones over there. There seems to be more this way." Jerry followed the pull. The moment the pond came into view, Gunter growled and fell back to Jerry's side. "I feel it too, boy."

"Feel what?"

"The energy shift." Jerry walked to the water's edge and looked out across the pond.

"Then the spirit is here?"

Jerry looked at Gunter for confirmation then shook his head. "Nope."

"It's almost dark. Ghosts like the dark, right?"

"Television ghosts like the dark. Real spirits don't have watches."

"Now what?"

"Now we try again tomorrow."

Sinclair grabbed Jerry's arm as he turned away from the pond.

Objecting to the handsy gesture, Gunter took Sinclair's arm in his mouth, applying just enough pressure to get the man's attention.

Sinclair pulled his arm free. "What was that?"

Jerry smiled. "You're a dog trainer. It was exactly what it felt like it was."

"I wanted to believe my little girl was telling the truth, but a part of me thought we were just out here wasting time. But I felt it, sure as if any of my dogs had placed their mouth on my arm. How is that even possible?"

"He was protecting me."

"From?"

"You."

"Me?"

"You put your hand on me."

"To get your attention!" Sinclair's voice rose a whole octave when he spoke.

"And lacking hands, Gunter used his mouth to get yours."

"It worked."

Jerry grinned. "I can tell."

"You're telling me that he's your bodyguard? I knew the military was experimenting with some crazy stuff, but Ghost Technology is beyond anything I ever imagined."

Gunter growled.

"I know, boy, I don't like it either. Gunter has nothing to do with my working for the agency."

Sinclair laughed. "The heck he doesn't."

Jerry sighed. "Okay, they brought me in because of Gunter, but he was already with me. The agency didn't have anything to do with it."

Sinclair paced back and forth in front of him. "Holy smoke, does your friend have any friends? We're talking stealth K-9 technology. Do you know the ramifications of that? Why, it could change the world."

"Don't get ahead of yourself, Sinclair. Gunter is the only one," Jerry said, hoping Fred hadn't let on to Houdini being Gunter's son.

"I don't believe you."

Gunter growled.

Jerry held up a hand to temper the dog. "My dog isn't all that thrilled you're calling me a liar."

"What? No, I didn't mean you. I meant mathematically; it doesn't make sense. If there is one, there has to be more."

The fur rose on Gunter's back as a throaty growl rumbled deep in his chest.

The hair on the back of Jerry's neck prickled. "He's near."

"Gunter? I know. I felt him."

"I'm talking about your spirit."

"Will that dog of yours protect me too?" It was obvious from the tremble in the man's voice he was now fully on board with believing in spirits.

"Just stay close." Jerry pulled Sinclair behind him and turned, picking his way back toward the pond. He stopped at the waterline and looked over the body of water. "It doesn't make sense."

"What doesn't?"

"The spirit is here, but I feel the bones we're looking for are in the pond."

"It makes perfect sense," Sinclair replied. "I put them there."

The spirit appeared and stood directly in front of Sinclair. "I should throw him in!" Standing just over six feet tall with a muscular build, the spirit looked more than capable of following through on his threat.

Sinclair rubbed his arms. When he spoke, his voice was barely above a whisper. "Did you feel that?"

"He's here."

"What does he want?"

"He's debating his options."

"Which are?"

"Top of the list seems to be wishing to throw you in the pond."

"Can he do that?"

"He seems to think he can."

"I don't get it. Why is he mad at me?"

Jerry held up a hand to silence the man and looked at the spirit. "I can help."

This time, Sinclair's voice was indignant. "You're offering to help him throw me in?"

"Shhh," Jerry shushed Sinclair then addressed the spirit. "If you tell me why you're so angry, I may be able to help."

"Why did he throw me in the pond? If he didn't

want my remains, he could have had the decency to bury them like he did the bones. I get that I don't get a proper burial. I knew that when I asked for my body to be donated to science."

"He said if you didn't want to use all the bones, you could have buried them instead of tossing them in the water," Jerry said, relaying the message to Sinclair.

"No, man, not bones. I'm talking the nitty gritty stuff that no one wants."

"I stand corrected. He said it wasn't bones you threw in the pond."

Sinclair's eyes grew wide. "If I weren't already a believer, I would be now. Listen, you have to make him believe me. I didn't discard them. I placed them with purpose so Maggie can find them. I know it seems as though I just tossed your remains down there to be used as fish food, but I promise you that couldn't be further from the truth. Forgive me for sounding crude, but the simple explanation is when a body decomposes, it puts off a gas. That gas is lighter than water and rises to the top of the pond. Maggie and dogs trained to do what she does are then able to locate the body."

Jerry cocked his head, listening to the spirit.

"What's he saying?"

"He said if you want to use a body, use a pig. He gave permission for his body to be used for science, not dog food," Jerry said, repeating the spirit.

Sinclair sighed. "Can he hear me?"

Jerry nodded. "He can."

Sinclair pulled himself taller. "Your body is being used for science and what can't be used or is no longer useful is shipped out to places where it can be of most use. Cadaver dogs are not born knowing what to do; they need to be trained. Unfortunately, there is only one way to train them, and that's by getting them used to the smell of decomposing bodies. Furthermore, if I were to use a pig, my dogs would be very adept at finding pigs."

"My dogs, and others like them, are being used to save lives and bring comfort to the living. Even though she is not fully certified, Maggie has already found three bodies in water and brought closure to those families. The dogs I've trained have found people buried in the rubble of the New York Trade Center, trapped under buildings after earthquakes, and lost in floods after tsunamis. They've helped find children and solved horrendous crimes. They've kept drugs from crossing the border and stopped bombs from getting onto flights. Dogs can predict seizures, sniff out cancer, lead the blind, warn the deaf, do chores for the disabled, and save children from drowning. I've even trained K-9 lifeguards to sit on the beach, so vacationers can enjoy their swim. And yes, I have trained dogs to sniff out bedbugs and termites. You may not have any use for dogs, but I assure you their usefulness has no limits. They say search and rescue dogs are the heroes, and I myself have received accolades for my work in training them, but the unsung heroes are people like you who selflessly donate your bodies to science so that we trainers can train the dogs."

Gunter barked as the spirit materialized for Sinclair to see.

"I…I can see him," Sinclair said, pointing to the man.

"This Maggie you speak of, she's the black German shepherd that rides in that little boat?"

Sinclair nodded.

"I won't be bothering her anymore."

"You mean she's not acting up because of hormones?"

"I may have scared her a time or two." The spirit shrugged. "I didn't know she was working; I thought she merely enjoyed taking a ride."

"So, we're good here?" Jerry asked.

"Almost," the spirit said.

"What else can I say?" Sinclair asked.

"Nothing, but I was wondering if you might consider naming one of the puppies after me."

Sinclair considered the request for a moment. "I could do that. What's your name?"

"Christopher."

Sinclair wrinkled his nose.

"My last name was Barkly," the spirit offered.

Sinclair bobbed his head. "That I can do."

"So, we're good?" Jerry repeated.

"Proceed with my blessing." Barkly turned and walked into the water.

"Is he gone?" Sinclair asked when the spirit disappeared.

"It's hard to tell, but I don't believe he will be of concern from here on out."

Sinclair shook Jerry's hand, pumping it up and down. "Boy, McNeal, not only did you solve my problem, but you made a true believer out of me."

They began walking back to the house with Gunter leading the way. "It is human nature to want to share this story with everyone you meet," Jerry said as they walked. "I can't stop you from telling people what happened here, but talking about Gunter is off-limits."

"It is? Can I ask why?"

"Only a handful of people know about him; otherwise, it would eliminate my element of surprise."

"I guess it would at that."

Jerry stopped and looked the man in the eye. "I'd be careful who you share any of this with."

Sinclair swallowed, sending his Adam's apple bobbing. "Because of the whole national security thing?"

"No, because of the whole people will think you're crazy thing. You have a good reputation in the field; if people start questioning your sanity, that might change."

Sinclair sighed, and they began walking once more.

Jerry could tell he'd burst the man's bubble. "If you ever feel the need to talk about spirits, give me a call. And if that little girl of yours tells you she sees something, believe her. If she asks questions you can't answer, bring them to me."

"Thanks, McNeal. I don't know how I could ever repay you."

"Jefferies sent me. This is on the company dime. I do have a favor to ask, though, if you could maybe find the time."

Sinclair's face lit up. "Anything, just say the word!"

"I met a boy in Pennsylvania who could use a little help with his dog."

"Your tone tells me there's a story behind the request. What's wrong with the dog?"

"No training. The kid is on the list for a dog, but apparently, those things take time. His dog looked young and healthy. I thought you might be able to help at least get the one he has under control." Jerry decided to be upfront with the man. "I nearly killed both of them when the boy followed the dog into the street."

"Give me the contact information. If I can't help them, I'll find someone who can."

"Good deal."

Gunter disappeared.

Jerry had a sinking feeling he knew where the dog had gone.

"The wife will be at her sister's for a few days. You're welcome to stay the night. We've got a spare room in the house, or you're welcome to use one of the bunk rooms if you'd like."

"Thanks for the offer, but my parents' house is only a couple hours' drive. I can't imagine being this close and not going home. The job keeps me on the road enough as it is." Plus, it would be good to get Gunter away from temptation – if it wasn't already too late.

"I know the truth," Sinclair said when they reached the Durango.

Jerry glanced in his direction. "About what?"

"Houdini."

Jerry worked to keep his voice even. "I don't know what you're talking about."

"We both know that's a lie. I thought the dog was just a superb animal, but now I know it was more than exceptional breeding. I saw how Maggie acted when you first arrived, and then you asked if she was in heat, as if there was a reason you wanted to know. It was because that dog of yours was sniffing around. I don't know the how of it, but I know that pup of yours was sired by that ghost dog. So what? Does that make him a half ghost or something? Don't worry; I'm not going to tell anyone," Sinclair said when Jerry failed to confirm his suspicions. "Like you said, no one would believe me if I did."

Jerry opened the door, slid into the driver's seat and started the engine without answering. *Come on, McNeal, would it kill you to give the man something?*

Sinclair's shoulders slumped as he turned and slowly walked toward the house.

Jerry powered down the window. "Sinclair!"

The man turned.

"You probably already know this, but you're a pretty smart man."

Sinclair took the comment for what it was and smiled.

***

Jerry pressed the button to call April.

"Hello."

"Hello, Beautiful. I just wanted to let you know I'm on my way home."

"Already?!"

"I can't tell if that is excitement or panic."

April giggled.

Instantly, the hairs on the back of his neck prickled. "What's wrong?"

"Nothing's wrong. It's been a good day."

Jerry drummed his fingers on the steering wheel. "Give me the highlights."

"I was going to wait until you got home, but I know you won't stop asking until I tell you."

"That's right, so spill it."

"I spoke to Harold."

"Is that name supposed to mean something?"

"Harold, as in Carol and Harold."

The tingle on his neck intensified.

"What happened?"

"Nothing happened. Not really anyway. I was in the pool when he showed up. I thought it was Mr. Bigsby, the man from Pennsylvania, because he showed up saying he wanted me to help his wife, but then he said he was looking for Carol, so I sent Mr. Bigsby away."

"Bigsby was there too?"

"Only because he thought I wanted him to be. I sent him away the moment I realized my mistake. I promised to help him, so I'm sure he'll be back."

"April?"

"Yes, Jerry?"

"Where were my parents when all this was going on?"

"Your dad was at the golf course and your mom was inside making cookies with Max."

Gunter woofed his approval.

"Hi, Gunter. Don't worry, they made extra."

Gunter licked his lips.

Jerry scowled at Gunter. "Don't count on getting any. April was dealing with spirits, and you were busy horn-dogging around."

Gunter smiled a K-9 smile.

"Are you saying…?"

"It's a good possibility."

"Maybe we should think about getting him neutered."

Gunter disappeared.

Jerry laughed. "I think you scared him. Tell me Houdini was with you."

"He was with me, but he didn't care about the spirits. He was too busy digging."

"Since when did he become a digger?"

"Since Harold buried forty-two thousand dollars in the dog run."

"Forty-two thousand? Are you sure?"

"Yep, your dad helped me count it."

"You told my dad about the money?"

"Of course. I needed a shovel to finish getting the capsule out of the hole."

"He was excited until I told him he couldn't keep it. Harold said he'd be back if that money didn't get to Carol."

Jerry could picture the look of disappointment on his father's face. "I'll bet."

"You said it was in the dog run?"

"Yes, it explains why Houdini kept nosing around back there."

"It does. I thought he was after the lizards."

"So did I. We need to learn to listen to him more. So that was my day. How was yours? Did you help Mr. Sinclair with his ghost problem?"

"One of them."

"Oh?"

"Yep, but something tells me we're going to make a believer out of his wife in a few months."

April laughed a carefree laugh.

"Hey, I don't like the idea of you being alone with the spirits. If this Bigsby fellow shows up, call for Gunter."

"I'm a big girl, Jerry."

"Please. Just until you get a handle on how this all works."

"Okay, Jerry."

"Thank you. I'll see you in a couple of hours."

"Love you."

"I love you too, Ladybug." Jerry ended the call and then dialed Sinclair's number.

"Mr. McNeal, did you change your mind about spending the night?"

"No. That thing we didn't talk about."

"Thing?"

"If Maggie ends up pregnant, I want the pick of the litter."

"Pick of the litter?"

"Isn't that the way it is usually done when using a stud dog?"

"Oh! Why yes, yes, it is."

The moment Jerry disconnected the phone, Gunter appeared and looked at him as if to say, *And just why do you need another dog?*

"I don't need another dog. April does. She had a spirit show up today – no, two," Jerry clarified. "Two spirits showed up, and neither you nor I knew anything about it until after the fact."

Gunter leaned back in the seat, looking at him as if to say, *You've been dealing with us all your life, and you turned out okay.*

"Yes, but this is April, and she's agreed to be my wife. How can I swear to protect her if I'm not there to do the job?" Jerry said in answer to the imagined comment.

Gunter yawned.

Jerry ran his hand over his head. "You're right. I'm getting ahead of myself. We don't even know if there will even be any more puppies. Maybe the other time was a fluke."

Gunter snorted.

"Pretty confident, old man."

Gunter licked his lips and answered with a K-9 grin.

The End

Will April be able to help Mr. Bigsby convince his wife the man she is dating isn't the man she thinks he is?

Will Jerry and April depart the ship as newlyweds?

Find out in Dearly Departed

Book 18 in the Jerry McNeal series.

Check out www.sherryaburton.com to sign up for my newsletter and order autographed copies, audiobooks, shirts, cups and more.

About the Author

Sherry A. Burton writes in multiple genres and has won numerous awards for her books. Sherry's awards include the coveted Charles Loring Brace Award, for historical accuracy within her historical fiction series, The Orphan Train Saga. Sherry is a member of the National Orphan Train Society, presents lectures on the history of the orphan trains, and is listed on the NOTC Speaker's Bureau as an approved speaker.

Originally from Kentucky, Sherry and her Retired Navy Husband now call Michigan home. Sherry enjoys traveling and spending time with her husband of more than forty years.